THE FUNERAL PORTRAIT

BY

VINCENT VIÑAS

Ink Smith Publishing
www.ink-smith.com

VINCENT VIÑAS

Printed in the U.S.A

ISBN: 978-1-939156-10-5

Ink Smith Publishing

P.O Box 1086

Glendora CA

www.ink-smith.com

THE FUNERAL PORTRAIT

For my parents

Day after day I feel no more alive than the stiff that lies the table before me. Reborn--unable to die. I've committed a hundred suicides.

-- Dog Fashion Disco

THINGS COULD BE BETTER

People don't care.

From the day you are born you are misled to believe you are loved. As you learn to stop shitting yourself, you are duped into thinking that your diaper is being changed out of affection. When you go to school, you are bamboozled into believing you are sitting in the corner, facing the wall for the rest of the afternoon because someone adores you enough to help you be a better person. As security escorts you from the job you have just been relieved of, you are spoon-fed the assurance that this experience builds character and it has nothing to do with you personally. It's just business. When your soul mate's lawyer sends you a restraining order because you won't stop telling them how much you miss them, some folks will tell you they feel for you and it's not your fault you are a pathetic loser who foolishly harbors hope.

THE FUNERAL PORTRAIT

When you're plummeting to the hard pavement from thirty stories above and that so-called "life" you led--or shall I say was led through--flashes before your tired eyes, you will see the truth. You will hear the screams of those around you--not shrieking because they give a damn you are about to become a bloody, shattered pâté on the sidewalk but because you are about to put a damper on their day, maybe even their week.

Having each floor represent one year of your lousy, pointless and unnoticed existence is as clever as you've ever been. No one will notice that. No one will make the connection. No one has ever connected with you, but at least you will see the truth and that's worth more to you than anything they've got. You'll see that people will put more effort into cursing you than greeting you. People will spit at you rather than kiss you. People will gladly push you down but not offer to pull you up onto your feet.

People will torture you slowly with insincerity, dishonesty, cruelty and hatred, while hoarding their love, care and admiration only for themselves. They will endlessly honor and celebrate their own lives and despise every breath that escapes your trembling lips. You will suffer miserably as you spiral towards your death. They will watch you die with wonder and enjoyment.

You are entertainment for their desensitized, warped minds to soak in over a low-carb T.V. dinner. A late summer re-run no one really has to pay much attention to because we've all seen this episode before. We've seen it countless times. Over and over and over until your life is nothing but a buzzing in someone's ear. White noise. And their finger is on the power

button ready to turn you off. Ready to shut you out. Ready to ignore you.
Ready to kill you.

People don't care. Why should you?

HOPE NEVER CRASHES MY PITY PARTY

APRIL 2ND

To My Dear Family,

After thirty years of heartache, disappointment and enough bullshit to fertilize the entire state several times over, I've decided I'm going to kill myself. This shouldn't come as much of a surprise to anyone. Maybe to you, Mom and Dad. You always thought I was a bit of an overly sensitive, downer and you know that I'm seeing that shrink but I'm sure you have no idea just how fucked up your son really is. See? I used the word "fuck." When have I ever used profanities in front of you? The truth is I use them all the time.

VINCENT VIÑAS

There's a lot you don't know about me and I'm very sorry that you'll never get the chance to find out more about how I really am. I prefer if you remembered me the way I was when I was a little boy. Not the spunkiest kid in the world but I was so much happier then. I'm sure I didn't look like it but I was--on the inside anyway. I still had a chance for the kind of life most people take for granted. I used to smile. I used to laugh. Now, the only time I laugh is when I can't believe how fucking crazy I am. And that kind of laughter always morphs into crying. You should see me. It's really pathetic. You'd be so ashamed that you'd wish I killed myself sooner.

I'm just a failed creation. It's not your fault. You loved me the best you could. I'm sorry you didn't get the little bundle of joy you deserved. People can be like any useless piece of shit item you might pick up in a department store clearance section—some come already broken and there are no refunds or exchanges. All births are final.

By the time you read this, I would have already plummeted to my death off the roof of the abandoned glass factory I sent you a picture of last year. Remember? I wrote that the factory reminded me of the photo you once showed me of Grandpa and his friends standing outside their old place of work. It's stupid really, now that I think about it. It's a fucking factory. Most of them look similar. I think I just mentioned that because I had nothing else to say. I guess I never really had much to say to either of you. I was never that great at verbalizing my thoughts or feelings on anything. You know that, so please don't be offended that this is most likely the longest conversation (albeit one-sided) we've ever had.

THE FUNERAL PORTRAIT

I've chosen to jump off of the glass factory for several reasons. Number one being that it's private. I don't want anyone to notice what I'm going to do and try to talk me out of it or physically stop me. I just want to be alone. If I wanted company I wouldn't be killing myself now, would I? The factory is also one of the tallest buildings in town. It's no skyscraper or anything but it should definitely do the trick with a head first dive. If by chance someone was driving by at that moment I wouldn't want to create a spectacle or give some poor soul nightmares so I'll be jumping down into the rear parking lot. I'll be sure to avoid landing in the handicap spot. That would be rude. Hey, you never know.

Prior to actually killing myself this time, I've stood at the ledge of the factory's roof before. From the ground, the building isn't that imposing but it's a long way down when you're up there. Long like a typical DMV visit. Long like an Oscar-thirsty, 18th Century, period piece that goes on forever until we can't cry anymore and we haven't the strength to further cheer the overcoming of oppression in one man's vision. I'm rambling I know. It's a long way down.

I've stood at that ledge more times than I care to remember, yet I can recount each visit clear as club soda without the bubbles. Just the very thought of it leaves a taste of melted luggage in my mouth. Or what I imagine melted luggage tastes like. I would often fool myself into thinking I was simply there for the view. It really is a beautiful view but most people who would go there for the scenic quality would enjoy it from inside the railing, not clutching the outside of it for dear life. Hmmm. Dear life... Excuse me while I address myself.

Dear Life,

It is with deep regret and excruciating anger that I must inform you that YOU SUCK! I have attempted to enjoy you for the better part of thirty years but you have made happiness an impossible task to fulfill. Apparently you are a gift – a precious prize I have been awarded, so I've been told many times. However, the alleged "gift" has so eloquently blossomed into a curse and I don't wish to possess it anymore.

It has gone from a delicious tray of scrumptious cookies to a filthy potato sack of rotten eggs. It has gone from a penthouse suite at the Bellagio to the janitor's closet at Bud's Rent-O-Room and Notary Public. This life has deteriorated from a stiff, eager erection to a droopy, pathetic mass of man-flesh with balls that hang so low they could almost be a tail.

So with all due respect, I hate you and I hope you die. I don't care to suffer anymore within your terms. I'm a grown man and can say with no outside influence that it is my intention to kill you. Perhaps you think you have more to offer me but how shall I say this... BULLSHIT!!! All the paint on my canvas has dried and cracked and the portrait you have crafted is one of sadness, failure, hopelessness and heartache so deep, I must be your masterpiece of sorry sacks of shit. Consider this my resignation, effective immediately. Thanks for nothing and here's hoping my relief is as swift as your punishment has been.

Sincerely and Bitterly,

Guy Edwards

THE FUNERAL PORTRAIT

P.S. In the event of reincarnation, if there is any way for someone to pick what he or she wishes to be in the next life then this is my formal request to come back as a doormat. I'd like to be of some use to someone the next time around. Thanks.

Sorry to interrupt my suicide letter with another sort of suicide letter but I felt compelled to let my life know how crappy it is, even if it was in an abstract fashion that would only make sense to a fucking lunatic.

So I will die like I've wanted to for a long time. I won't lie, if things had worked out differently with Constance I probably wouldn't be doing this, but I'd never blame her. I don't want anyone to blame her. It's not her fault we didn't work out. I wouldn't want to be with me either.

I'm sure that will piss you off, Bruno, because I know you think my demeanor is all attributed to her, but like I've already pointed out to Mom and Dad, I've always been like this. Besides, you're better off not having me as your brother. You always did say I was an embarrassment to the family. Just pretend I never existed and you should be okay. I know you'll miss hitting me in the face with pies when I come home but I'm sure you'll find something else to occupy your time. You're a creative guy.

I'm going to stand on the ledge of the factory with my favorite picture-- together with Constance--in one pocket and the Zippo lighter she gave me in the other. I'll spread my arms and just wait for the perfect breeze to come along and nudge me forward to my death. That's another reason I've chosen the factory. I am scared, there's no denying it. I could never put a gun to my

11

head, slit my wrists or hang myself. I'm way too much of a pussy for stuff like that.

On the factory ledge I can just stand there until I'm ready and when I am, with just a little lean, my body will be drawn to the hard ground below. Then it will be over and I'll be free. It's all I've ever wanted, to be free of this sadness that has taken up residence in my heart since I was born. If I can't find freedom in life, then I will seek it out in death. I love you and I'm so sorry for any pain I may have caused you.

With all that's left of my love,

Guy

APRIL 3RD

To My Dear Family,

I had planned to kill myself yesterday and I don't really feel like writing out a whole new suicide letter explaining why so I'll thank you to read the previous one first and then this one afterwards.

As you can see I chickened out. It was wishful thinking but I knew it wasn't going to happen yesterday. That's what makes the situation all the more pathetic. I know every time I stand out on that ledge that it isn't going to happen. I want it to though--really bad. So much that it hurts. But it just wasn't in the forecast. Damn, even the realization that I can't stop being a coward long enough to jump isn't enough to inspire me.

Things weren't always like this. Things were better a million years ago it seemed. It's next to impossible to remember but I once smiled on a voluntary basis. It didn't hurt to smile then. It felt good to smile, to laugh-- to not want to die every second of every hour of every fucker of a day.

Mrs. Herman, the widow down the street, who has more cats than the average ten animal shelters combined and who smells like year old orange peels told me that it took more energy to frown than it did to smile. Sure, she

13

lost her husband of forty years and replaced him with a litter of cats that rivals the population of most gypsy campsites. And okay, once in a while she forgets her husband is dead and traps me by the mail box for over an hour, filling me in on the details of the surprise birthday party she is throwing him. I usually just promise to bring the potato salad and never show up. No one does. Not me. Not any of the neighbors. And especially not her husband.

But still, what does she know about pain? True pain. I hate to sound so dramatic but I'm fairly certain the melancholy that haunts me is the worst ever known to man. It has to be, because the thought that someone is worse off than me makes me feel selfish for being so down. Its way easier to wear the "Hi, I'm the World's Most Miserable Bastard" tag than it is to admit someone else's shit-storm has a stronger wind-chill than mine. And maybe that crazy old cat lady is right. Maybe it did take more energy to frown than it did to smile, but that's only if you smile naturally. The kind of smiling I'm doing these days, that forced, I wish I was dead, smiling you have to do so people stop asking you what's wrong, is tough. That kind of smiling is harder than anything a facial contortionist can come up with.

So I'm going back to the ledge with my picture and lighter. I really love that picture of Constance and me. It's all bent because it's always in my pocket every time I try to take a flying leap. Don't people always say that to someone who they don't like? Go take a flying leap? I actually am trying to. Maybe I should take a long walk off a short pier instead. That might work out for me, although drowning sounds horrible. Or worse, a hungry shark might come along, tear off one of my legs and then I'll drown while bleeding to death in tremendous pain. Yikes!

THE FUNERAL PORTRAIT

I can't believe my hand still trembles when I hold that picture up to look at it. Constance is so beautiful. Beautiful with a touch of heartless bitch. She's the kind of person who always gets what she wants and can't deal with something she doesn't want, that in turn doesn't want to go away—namely, me. I have so little of her left in my life. That's why I cherish the Zippo lighter so much. It's the only thing she's ever given me. Bruno, I know you said she's a "deranged cunt" for giving me a lighter, even though I don't smoke, but that doesn't matter. What matters is that I wanted a lighter. I just like Zippos and I never had one. She filled that void in my life. Oh sure, that's like a micro-void but if you've ever felt emptiness--vicious, never ending emptiness--you'd be grateful to fill even the most minuscule amount in some way.

I have to be honest and tell you this probably won't be my last letter to you. I do plan to kill myself today but I know what will most likely occur. I will stand on that ledge, clutching my lighter to the spot on my chest where my heart had once resided—desperation leaking from my eyes. I will tell myself it just isn't time yet to die and then slowly climb back over to the side of the ledge where people who don't want to fall to a horrible death stand.

The usual wave of relief will then make its way through me as I sit on the roof, out of harm's way. This wave will shortly be followed by another one full of self-pity that usually comes crashing down pretty fucking hard. An hour later I would be so motivated to go through with it that I would go marching right back to that ledge and take a swan dive if it weren't for the fact that I have to clean my bathroom or rearrange my sock draw or blah, blah, blah. Routine is a great thing when you feel like crap. It provides less of a chance to think about the cancer in your heart. I know I said a heart no longer resides in my chest but that can't be true. It has to be in there. What else could this pain be?

I love you all and I hope you understand,

Guy

APRIL 4TH

To My Dear Family,

Something incredibly strange happened yesterday during my suicide attempt. There I was, up on the roof, heading for my usual spot on the ledge--I can't believe that's my usual spot now. What kind of a fucking maniac have I become? Anyway, as I got near the ledge I noticed a dark red piece of construction paper taped to the railing. It was a note in black ink which read "Are you lost? Let us find you" in what I have to admit was a very attractive handwriting. Probably a woman's. I don't think a man is capable of such a lovely font.

Naturally I freaked out when I saw this note and spent the next hour searching the factory and surrounding area to see if I was being followed or watched in any way. I didn't find any evidence of anyone else being there at all. No other cars. No footprints. Not even tire marks. Nothing. It was like a ghost had placed the note there. Perhaps someone who used to work at that factory and met their end there the same way I'm trying to. And as you can guess, this thought gave me such a case of the creeps that I couldn't haul ass out of there fast enough once I thought it. In doing so I managed to snag my pants on a nail or something. It ripped them open enough in the back that you could see my underwear, which unfortunately were a pair of boxers covered in little drawings of rabbits.

I like bunnies, okay, Bruno? You bring all types of weird creatures and animals home from your job all the time so I don't think my boxers are a big deal. And might I add, I find it amazing that you seem to work at the only pet store in Florida that doesn't have a single goddamn bunny in stock, ever! I think you purposely don't order them because I like them. You have a different snake for every day in the month but God forbid you get a little Netherland Dwarf or Lop in there some time.

Before I get even more off subject let me get back to what I was saying. So I found this mysterious note, which I'm sure was either placed there by a person way before I showed up or the day before and was not conjured by a deceased factory worker. I'm still spooked by it, though. Not so much by the cryptic nature of the note but by the fact that someone was watching me for who knows how long. This amazingly private and convenient spot I had found to kill myself was now compromised. Tainted.

But then I thought perhaps whoever put this note there was a very religious person trying to help me. Don't people usually turn to religion when they feel lost or are in despair? It could have just been a very vague pamphlet of some sort, but don't they typically say something like let Jesus find you or let God find you? Who the hell is us? That's what's bothering me. Now, I'm not going to let them spoil my suicide because I've been keeping that ledge company far too long to just go deserting it for any reason less than my horrific end.

In fact, I hope whoever left that note comes back while I'm there. I will make them wish they never found my ledge. I will ensure that the image of my falling body hitting the ground below in a bloody, twisted mess will haunt their dreams each and every night for the rest of their days.

That's what I want to do. This is so hard and it just got harder. Goddamn it, why can't I just kill myself?

I love you.

Guy

VINCENT VIÑAS

APRIL 9TH

To My Dear Family,

I have let a few days go by since the "note" incident and I am, once again, ready to kill myself. I am so sick of this life I can't even put it into words. Maybe if I just spat blood onto a page that might begin to cover how I feel right now. Regular tears aren't cutting it for me these days. I want to cry blood. There's all this blood in me and I want it out. It's keeping me alive and I hate it. I fucking hate this blood. I can feel it pumping in my veins, making its way back and forth through my body, telling me that there's life there but I don't feel the life. I just feel the blood. And if I can't feel that life too then I don't want even a drop of this fucking blood in me. Let it leave me so that this useless life that comes with it can leave me too.

In case it's not painfully obvious, I've been severely miserable since my last letter. I've just been dragging myself around like a collection of bones and organs in an epidermis bag. I mean, no one expects me to show up for work singing and dancing, given the nature of my job, but even my demeanor is starting to depress our customers more than their losses. I guess it's kind of dumb when you think about it. Why would someone like me, who wants

20

nothing more than to be dead, choose a career as a Funeral Director? I think maybe it's because I'm such a chickenshit when it comes to my own death that I feel the need to be surrounded by people who have achieved what I desire most. I know...stupid.

But I keep dragging my ass to work every day to hang out with the lucky sons of bitches who won't ever have to renew their licenses again or pick out throw pillows that perfectly accent their new couch. This is my daily routine. Wake up in the morning, take a shower, get dressed, have a cup of coffee, read the newspaper, almost kill myself, take a nice walk, go to work.

Today is such a beautiful day too for people who, unlike me, have the strength to lift their heads towards the sky. That's why I enjoy bad weather so much. The falling rain, hitting the pavement, gives me something extra to look at when my eyes are buried in the ground. I wish the rest of me could be buried in the ground.

I don't know why I feel the need to point out that I just sighed very heavily but I did.

Well, I'm off to the factory to kill myself. This time I'm going to do it. And if whoever left that note is on the roof there's no way they're going to talk me out of it. I am lost, I'll give them that much, but I don't need them to find me. I want something else to find me. I'm right here waiting for it, waving a huge white flag. If you could pray for such a thing, I'd pray for the Angel of Death to find me and wrap its black wings around my body until there was nothing left but the fleeting, insignificant, yet bitter tasting, memory of the poor excuse for a man, known as Guy Edwards. I sighed again. I do that a lot.

VINCENT VIÑAS

It's not fair,

Guy

THE FUNERAL PORTRAIT

APRIL 10TH

Dear Mom and Dad,

I was all set on killing myself yesterday but I decided to stop by work first. I had left some quiche in the office refrigerator about a week ago and meant to throw it out before it started to smell. When you work at a funeral home, you don't want things to start smelling rotten or people might easily get the wrong idea. In the grand scheme of things, who the hell cares about some stupid quiche stinking up the place? I should have been more concerned with creating my own rotten smell from my dead body lying out in the hot Florida sun for a couple of days before someone found whatever the buzzards didn't finish yet. That was harsh. I'm sorry.

As I began driving off for the factory I spotted Mr. Friar sitting on the side of the road with his peaches. I think I've mentioned him to you before. His name is Eric Friar and he lives in one of the retirement communities down the road from my job. Occasionally, he sits out on the road selling peaches he gets from his son's produce company. He doesn't have to. I think he does it just to have something different to do once in a while. He would always say he wasn't really just selling peaches but was guarding the road to the retirement community. Not from people trying to get in, but from the old farts trying to get out and plaguing the world with soiled underpants in need of changing; that mothball smell of their clothes; years of coffee breath and endless tales of grandchildren who never visit. His little peach stand also gave him a chance to converse with new people and keep an upbeat energy, which he said the other museum pieces he lived amongst lacked.

I've stopped to buy peaches from him several times and we've become friends. Foolishly, most of my purchases were at Bruno's request, which he in turn used to make peach cobblers. As you can imagine, many of those peach cobblers ended up smack in the face of yours truly.

I've always admired Friar's positive outlook on life. Our conversations are usually head on collisions of old optimism and young pessimism but I try to stop and chat with him whenever I can. I always wonder if the old man could tell just a short time prior to our talks, most days, I had almost plunged to my death. As if old people had a sixth sense for suicidal tendencies like a horse can see a ghost in the road. Probably not. But I'm sure the old man is doing me more of a favor by being my friend than I am being his.

Friar was doing a little meditating before the big senior's checkers tournament in between selling those peaches. The tournament was big, not the seniors. He asked me how was doing. I couldn't think of anything to say other than "I'm still alive", which came out with all the enthusiasm of week-old road kill. "Is that good or bad?" he responded. I guess I haven't quite figured that one out yet. Friar must think I'm easier to read than a pop-up book because he changed the subject right away.

He asked me if I replaced those pants I ripped the other day (I stopped by afterwards to pick up peaches for Bruno) or if I had just fixed them. I didn't tell him what I was doing prior to tearing those pants. I didn't want to open that barrel of worms—my issues don't fit in a can anymore. Friar then told me that he compared love to a pair of pants. I thought this was perhaps senility settling in but he made sense.

He says, "Finding love is like finding the right pair of pants. You try on all different types until you find that perfect fit. You grow to love and depend on those pants until eventually they wear out from use. However, the right pair of pants can last a lifetime if you take care of them. Unfortunately though, there are times, without warning, where you can lose your pants and unexpectedly find yourself outside with your dick in the dirt. You can never be prepared for that."

I can't really say I understood the last part so I chalked up that little tidbit to senility or perhaps he had just been out in the sun too long. A bit odd and confusing, yes, but I found it to be compelling advice. I promised him I'd immediately start looking for a new pair of "pants."

He told me to start looking right away because the monks were full of shit—solitude was overrated. And that's why I usually stop by Mr. Friar's peach stand to begin with. He's typically a nice, swift and positive slap to the face. Caffeine for the soul. It's like he knows what I'm thinking without me having to say it and he tells me what I want to hear. I guess I'm just that easy to read, which really depresses me further if that's the case.

Maybe I'm not a pop-up book after all. Maybe I'm more like a coloring book instead. Page after page of boring black and white just dying for someone to come along and add some color to my life. No, I'm an activity/coloring book. That's more like me. I'm a page of endless letters. There are words in there somewhere. There's meaning. You just need to find it and make sure you circle it so you remember where it is. I'm barely a person until you connect the dots and see me standing there with that catastrophic look of selfish misery. I'm two pictures side by side and you need to spot the differences between them. In picture number one Guy is smiling. In picture number two Guy is smiling because he has just blown his brains out.

I want to die...I think.

Sincerely,

Guy

APRIL 11TH

Dear Bruno,

My dear brother, I'm sorry to leave you without a sibling but you should know better than anyone how miserable I am since we live together. You probably wouldn't think you're to blame for any of my depression anyways but I'd still like to take this opportunity to say my death isn't your fault. I know we haven't seen eye to eye on everything in our lives. You seem to have the ability to always come out on top, regardless of the situation or what you actually did or didn't do. Like the time Mom and Dad came to visit and the place was a wreck because you didn't clean, even though I asked you to, and you told them it was my fault because I didn't remind you what day they were coming. They really bought that one.

Or the time you made it seem like I only eat drive-through fast food for every meal because I didn't bring you any that one day and I had to listen to a two hour lecture from Dad on eating healthy, even though, not only do I not eat fast food every day, but I'm also a grown man and could eat whatever the fuck I want if I feel like it. They didn't see it that way though because Bruno's word--your word--is gold. Always. No matter what I say or do. It's not fair really but there's no changing it so I'm not holding that against you anymore.

Even the whole pie thing has grown on me. I used to be so annoyed by it, to the point I've contemplated stabbing you in your sleep or maybe just re-arranging everything in your room while you were out (I know that would drive you out of your fucking mind) but I just learned to live with it. Because when your older brother hits you in the face with a pie every other time you walk through the front door, eventually you stop getting annoyed by it and you start wondering where the hell is he getting all of these pies from?

Does he have a secret storage somewhere in his room? Does he scurry down to the market whenever you leave the house to get one and then waits anxiously by the door for your return? Maybe he even makes them himself each time, although (as any Three Stooges fan can tell you) putting together anything more complicated than a simple whipped cream pie is worth eating instead. I know you would never reveal your secret so I won't ask, but if there was a world ranking for something like that you'd easily be number one. It's frightening to even consider that there might be someone else on Earth who is better at the pie thing than you.

I was a bit peeved about the Pecan pie you hit me with last week though, because you know not only am I allergic to Pecan pie but especially crappy Pecan pie like the one you threw. And whatever portions fell off of my face seems to have left what looks like a bleach stain on my shirt. What the hell was in that pie? Plus, getting the gooey mess of Pecan pie out of my eyes is harder than wiping away, say, Blueberry or Apple pie so I only got to hear you choking with laughter.

I didn't get the whole visual experience of my ridicule. I especially enjoy the part where you point as if the room were full of people who needed help in identifying who it was to be laughed at, mockingly. And, as I knew would inevitably happen, my face swelled up like a pack of hotdogs within an hour or so.

You then asked, and I quote, "So what's my shit stain of a brother doing today?" Such a smoothie, you are. I told you I was going to see Constance before the Pecan pie made my face resemble that of the Elephant Man. You didn't even finish swallowing the orange juice you were drinking, straight out of the carton I might add, when you stomped over to me. The conversation went something like this:

"What in fuck's sake are you going to see that bitch for?" As splashes of the still yet to be swallowed orange juice in your mouth landed, appropriately of course, on me. I told you I had no answer, other than I just wanted to see her, which is always my answer. You came back with, "Don't you have a brain, spaghetti dick? That girl is the reason you're all out of whack and you keep giving her more chances to screw you up. Get over it already!" But you don't understand, Bruno. We're really just friends. Maybe you don't believe that. Shit, maybe I don't believe it but it's what I'm sticking with because if Constance and I aren't friends then we aren't anything. And I can't bear the thought of that.

That didn't stop you there though. "Please." (pronounced Puh-Leez) "I see you, Guy. Always looking at her picture and carrying around that stupid lighter she gave you, which to me just shows how fucked up in the head she

29

is because you don't even smoke." I'm shocked you passed up the chance to call her a deranged cunt again. But like I've told you countless times, I just wanted a lighter. "You're even wearing that watch that you bought her that she gave back." That's true. I have been the wearing the Swatch watch I bought her when I went to New York. She's allergic to the plastic armband, you know that. I thought she was kidding but it's true and besides, I needed a watch anyways.

"I'm tempted to pull down your pants right now to see if you're wearing a pair of her panties." I know my first instinct was to quickly move a few steps away from you when you said that but it's not because you were right. I just didn't want you trying to forcibly find out. I'm sure you thought you were correct in your assumption though, given your response. "You're pitiful, man. Maybe you two psychos deserve each other. Go! Just go and see your psycho ex-girlfriend and when she rips you apart again, don't expect any sympathy from me."

I don't want your sympathy, Bruno. I just want you to understand where I'm coming from. It's a dark, lonely, miserable place from where I'm reaching out to you. I know I can't make you think of Constance in any other light than you currently do, but I want you to know how troubled I am. Was. So maybe you won't hold some things against me. Like I said, it's not sympathy I'm after. I don't expect sympathy from anyone. And I don't give a shit what you think of my decisions.

Whether you think they are wrong or right, I just want you to understand why I made them. This is my life and if it's a mess then it's my mess. I had to write this to you before I died because I wasn't sure if you were listening when

30

this actually happened. The reason I think that you might not have been paying super close attention to what I was saying is due to that second pie you hit me with just before I left. Getting hit again wasn't much of a surprise but the fact that you practically pulled it out of thin air was shocking. You are getting way too good at that. I will miss the punishment. I didn't mean to complain so much. I just wanted to tell you what was on my mind before I ended it all.

Take care of yourself and all those animals, Bro.

Guy

SANITY HAS LEFT THE BUILDING

APRIL 15TH

To My Dear Family,

I don't even know where to begin. My quest for death has taken such an unexpected, such an unheard of turn, that I think perhaps instead of depression, it's insanity that has infested me. It couldn't have been a dream because there's hard evidence to suggest otherwise. That's what scares me even more, the fact that I know what happened was very real and I can't imagine any logical explanation for it. I am almost too terrified to be sad right now. I'm shivering just recounting the day's events in my head, but I feel like I need to tell you what happened for this could very well be the last letter I write you. I might not die like I planned but this could be my final day as an otherwise sane person.

I hadn't forgotten about the note I found on the factory rooftop but it wasn't tugging at my paranoia like it had in the days following. So I found myself on that ledge again with a fresh sadness due to an encounter with Constance. Well, it wasn't really an encounter because she doesn't know I saw her. I went to the mall to see a movie by myself. Sometimes I go see comedies during opening weekends. No matter how funny the movie is to the rest of the crowd it never manages to get a laugh out of me. I just go because being around other people while they laugh makes me feel like a part of society in some small way. It also reminds me that happiness is possible, even if for only ninety minutes. I know, it's a stupid logic, but in my defense I am a very troubled person.

On the way out of the mall, I noticed Constance through the window of a clothing store. She was with a friend and they were holding different articles of clothing up against themselves in front of a mirror, the typical way a woman does when they don't want to actually try on an outfit but want to get an idea of how they'd look in it. She looked very happy. Her and her friend seemed to be sharing a laugh a minute, but in this case a minute was about five seconds long. And it made me think, how come she can laugh and carry on and be so happy just looking in a stupid mirror, trying on clothes in a half-ass manner while I'm walking around praying for the end of the world? At first it made me mad but by the time I got to my car I was near tears. The only thing I could think to do was drive right over to the factory and finally do what I should have done a long time ago.

A short time later I was standing on the rooftop ledge, completely consumed with sadness. I was sure this would be it. After a few moments though I looked off to the side and noticed a young woman was standing there, leaning against the inside of the railing. She was smiling at me and I realized at that moment that she had been talking but I had blocked it out. The woman was attractive in a ghostly kind of way, with fiery, blood red hair and burnt out eyes surrounded by black makeup that matched her dress. Either it was unexpectedly October 31st or she was one of these "Gothic" girls. It made no sense to me for someone who looked like sunlight would kill them to live in Florida. I'm sure the "Sunshine State" is hardly on any vampire's vacation agenda.

When she spoke, her voice was unlike anyone's I've ever heard in person. It reminded me of one of those actresses from the 1940s with its deep and rich smokiness. It was a "lady's" voice and it didn't suit her. Well, at first it didn't suit her but overall I guess it did, I just didn't expect it. "Hey, buddy?" That's what she was saying. I was beyond frazzled but that was quickly overtaken by annoyance. How dare she interrupt my suicide? That's exactly the kind of thing I'd expect from Constance. And where the hell did this woman come from? Was she the one who left that note? I should tell her to fuck off, double-time. However, all I could get out was a shrewd "What do you want?"

She asked if I had a light. I didn't realize until then that a cigarette was pursed between her icy lips, bouncing up and down as she spoke. I had my lighter but I told her "no" and to "go away." Then she had the nerve to ask me what I was doing? I didn't lie. I told her I was going to kill myself. Perhaps that would scare her off, I hoped, but she didn't flinch at all. She simply asked,

"Why?" So I told her it was none of her business and repeated my request for her to go away.

Out of the corner of my eye I could see her lean over the railing, surveying the distance to the ground. "Are you sure you don't have a light?" I just wanted to get rid of her so I angrily hopped over the railing and back onto the roof. I lit her cigarette with my lighter and she took a long drag off of it, really savoring the nicotine. Then after thanking me she asked if she could bum a cigarette off of me as well. I told her that I didn't smoke so she pointed out the fact I carry a lighter. At that moment I pointed to the watch on my wrist (the one I had bought Constance) and I told her, "I'm also wearing a woman's watch, but wearing a woman's watch doesn't make me a lady anymore than carrying a lighter makes me a smoker. Have a good day."

I climbed back over the railing, sure that she would finally bug off but it wasn't meant to be. She called out again, "Hey?" I asked her, "What do you want now?" while putting on my best fed up facial expression.

"You got a name?" I told her my first name. "That's a really nice lighter, Guy." I thanked her. "Can I keep it?" What?! No! "Why not? You're just gonna kill yourself anyway." I didn't go into detail but I told her that I wanted a certain someone to know I had it with me when I died. Very casually she responded, "I see. Well, do you mind if I finish this cigarette here while you kill yourself?" I told her with an even better fed up face and matching tone to do whatever she wanted but to just leave me alone. "That's cool." What the hell was wrong with this woman?

Naturally, she kept talking and our exchange went something like this.

35

"You know, I hate to butt in but statistics show that if you haven't jump by now you don't really want to." You don't know anything.

"I'm not trying to belittle your efforts, pal. I'm just saying." Well, don't say anything. I'm in pain.

"Hey, we're all in pain, Guy. You. Me. Even whoever's responsible for your being up here." Yeah, maybe.

"Do you really want to die?"

No one had ever asked me that point blank. It caught me by surprise and I couldn't answer right away. She noticed my hesitation before I finally said yes.

"Let's find out."

Before her words could even sink in she quickly moved closer to me and did something I would never have imagined her doing. She grabbed my ass. Instinctively, my body jerked forward and I lost my balance. I began to fall forward and a panic I could never put into words swept through me. Desperately, I reached behind me and was able to grab onto the bottom portion of the railing. I almost lost my grip when my body swung and hit against the building with a thud, not unlike a pillowcase of ground beef falling off of a table. (I should really work out before I kill myself. I'm so out of shape.)

In my terror I looked up to see the woman, leaning over the railing and peering down at me. Wouldn't you fucking believe it, the bitch was smiling. I wanted to grab her by her pale neck and fling her off the roof to watch her fall to her stupid death. Then I'd let go of the railing and I would land on her

36

twisted body to make sure she's dead, killing myself in the process. That would work. If only she was within grabbing distance. Instead, she began another conversation as I hung there, struggling to climb back up.

"Isn't this fun?" Are you crazy?!

"Is that any way to talk to someone who is trying to do you a favor?" A favor?! You're trying to kill me!

"But don't you want to die?" Yes!

"Then what's the problem?"

She tossed her lit cigarette down at my face and I lost my grip on the railing with one hand. I screamed like a little girl. I'm not proud of that but I'm trying to be honest here. As soon as I regained my grip we were able to finish our lovely conversation.

Not like this! I don't want to die like this! "How then?"

I don't know! "But you do want to die, correct?"

Yes! Now please help me up. "All right."

I held on while she rummaged through her coffin-shaped purse for something. After a few moments she produced a pair of handcuffs that I could only imagine had been for the purpose of shackling her boyfriends to some godforsaken Count Dracula bedpost while things like candle wax, whips, blood, skulls and other unholy sexual knick-knacks were put to excruciating use. I must have made a face because she gave the handcuffs a second glance and then told me not to judge her. She dangled one end towards me and suggested that I grab hold of it so she could pull me up. I had to totally disregard the potential history of those handcuffs' whereabouts just to be able to touch them with my bare hand.

In no time at all I was back on the roof, panting heavily and confronted now by something worse than death--this especially strange woman who in a minute's time tried to take and then saved my life. Even if I could speak through the jagged breathing, I had no idea what to say.

"My name is Tallulah. Tallulah Leigh." Still out breath, I told her my full name. "Nice to meet you, Guy Edwards. I think we can help each other." I couldn't imagine in what way we could do that. She insisted we go grab a bite to eat and I was reluctant so she chimed in with, "Oh, come on. It's not gonna kill you." I thought this was a poor choice of words given what just transpired on the ledge. She knew what she was saying because she smiled and told me that was a joke. I very dryly told her it was funny and she said, "Just a barrel of laughs, I am. Come on."

I watched her start to walk away and for reasons I couldn't even figure out myself, I followed her. When I finally made my way outside, this woman, Tallulah, was sitting on the hood of my car, waiting. I didn't see any other cars around so I asked her where she was parked. She told me that she didn't drive to the factory but had in fact flown there on a broomstick. A very sly grin accompanied this proclamation but I have to admit, given her behavior and appearance, I wouldn't have been too surprised if this were true.

A short time later we were sitting in a Cracker Barrel restaurant, which was unusually empty but I figured that was due to the violent storm that was about to pick up outside. Tallulah let me buy her a box of chewy cinnamon

38

candy, which she managed to polish off even before our real food arrived. She kept going on about how much she loved that all the candy at Cracker Barrel came in vintage packaging. I bought some chocolate-covered nougat, which I actually forgot I had and they got all melted in the car later so I ended up tossing them out.

Tallulah also insisted on getting a hand buzzer from the jokes and novelties section of their store/waiting area. If I had a nickel for every time she buzzed me with that thing within five minutes of having it, all that change could have covered our meal, candy, a quarter tank of gas and the buzzer itself.

I was still too upset and weirded out to have much of an appetite, but Tallulah scarfed down her country fried steak meal and mine so nothing went to waste. Either she hadn't eaten in days or her metabolism was faster than the speed of light because she was a thin girl. Her Goth look definitely did not blend in with the Country-style atmosphere of the place, either. It was as if Morticia Addams made a guest appearance on Little House on The Prairie.

In between bites of food she blurted out an endless supply of questions that I ignored. She would respond to them herself with short one word answers, like "cool", "sweet" or "neat." Finally she asked, "So what's your story?" and I told her I didn't have one. "Cute." I couldn't hold back anymore and I demanded to know why she didn't just let me jump off the roof the way I wanted to. "You're not still upset about that, are you?" I started to talk but didn't really know what I wanted to say. She knew what I was thinking though.

Tallulah knew that I wanted to end it all but just couldn't seem to cross that line and how frustrating it was. "Well, then perhaps it's fate that we met." I didn't know what she meant. She leaned over the table a bit closer and softly said, "Just between you and me, I want to end it all too." I asked her why, but she suggested I go first. I didn't want to talk about it so Tallulah said we could engage in some typical getting to know you, bullshit, chit-chat for a bit instead. I can't tell you how confused I was by this woman.

I'm not exactly sure how typical getting to know you, bullshit, chit-chat goes but this is how ours went:

"So what do you do for a living, Guy?"

Do you wanna hear what I really do for a living or do you wanna hear what I tell people to impress them?

"What do you say to impress them?"

I say I'm a Poet/Novelist/Screenwriter/Songwriter.

"Wow. That is impressive."

Thanks. I used to tell women I was a Funeral Director.

"Did that work?"

Only with the living dead.

"Nice. So what do you really do,

Mr.Poet/Novelist/Screenwriter/Songwriter?"

I'm a Funeral Director.

"Sweet."

Yeah, it's not glamorous but its steady work.

"Of course. I'm sure you have loads of customers just dying for your services."

That's funny.

"That's the second time I've been funny and you've yet to laugh."

Ha.

"That's a start."

Tallulah then started telling me how she thought Funeral Directors were sexy, which didn't surprise me based on her looks and coffin-shaped purse. Then she wanted to know if I was ready to share the reason why after spending all of my time around dead people, I was so anxious to bunk with them on the embalming table so badly. I didn't want to tell her though. She had asked too many questions already. It was fine with her that I still didn't want to share the source of my suicidal tendencies but she insisted I allow her to ask four more questions. I was so annoyed at this point that I agreed and let her know I would be leaving immediately after her final mini-interview.

Her first question was if I found her attractive. I wasn't expecting that so I had a kind of delayed reaction. I wanted to lie and say no, but I couldn't. Despite the fact she looked like she might not have a pulse and lives in a cemetery she was attractive. Even more so than I had initially thought, really.

The second question was if I found her sexually attractive. I thought this was a given after the first question but I realize now that attractive and sexually attractive can be two separate things. Part of me wanted to survey her figure but she never broke eye contact and I would've felt like a pervert, staring at her chest while she watched me closely.

I didn't need to do that though since after giving it a little thought I could recall her physical makeup perfectly. She was a thin girl, but not skinny if that makes sense. Her black dress, which also had a gray pattern on it, wasn't form fitting but was tight enough to notice how shapely she was. Tallulah definitely had curves where the average superficial male required them to be. Her skin was pretty pale, so I wondered if she lived in Florida at all or if she really had arrived on that broomstick she mentioned, possibly from some mythical realm with an endless supply of overcast skies.

The light tone of her complexion brought to mind the cadavers I dealt with at work. Her lips had a touch of blue to them as if she had been suffering from hypothermia earlier in the day. Everything about her (aside from the curves) was not what usually caught my attention, yet something in me wanted her at that moment. I was even without an inkling of Constance in my thought process while staring into Tallulah's haunting dark eyes that I just then noticed were a midnight green. Yes, I was sexually attracted to her and let her know in a rather shy way, trying to be nonchalant. She didn't blink.

"If I asked you to go outside, behind the building with me, so we can make out, would you?" was the third question. I didn't want to let on how hypnotized she made me by this notion but it was damn near impossible. I was at a loss for words and had to hold onto the table to keep from shaking. She waited for my answer, quietly, and still, without blinking. I couldn't say that I would turn down the offer was my response.

Never in my life have I ever interacted in such a way with a strange woman that I had just met. You know me. I'm not the one night stand, love'em and leave'em type. I like to get to know someone first before I even suggest anything remotely intimate. But I kid you not when I say I felt powerless to her aura. There was no denying it. She had me and I didn't know what to do with myself. I think I even thought for a second if maybe she had slipped some sort of witch's love potion in my soda while I wasn't looking but that seemed unlikely.

Then Tallulah hit me with her final question, which I knew was coming but I still wasn't ready for as it traveled from her frosty looking lips to my ringing ears. "Do you want to go outside, behind the building with me, so we can make out?" Like some old monster movie, as if on cue, heavy thunder rumbled somewhere in the (not too far) distance as soon as she spoke the words. The rain was coming down harder now and normally in this type of weather I always felt it was best to stay indoors. Never mind getting soaked. I was more concerned with getting struck by lightning.

The weather's turn for the worse had no effect on Tallulah as she just stared at me, patiently awaiting the outcome of her final question. I peered out the window for what seemed like awhile. You could barely see the cars parked just five feet away through the rain. I looked back at Tallulah. Who was this woman? And why was I about to pay our check, walk out the door, head around back and suck on her lips in such dangerous, hurricane-type rain? I didn't know. I still don't but I couldn't pay that check fast enough.

I know you would say I'm an idiot, Bruno, for engaging in such activities with someone I don't even know, but there I was--in the pouring rain with lightning all around the area, tongue wrestling with this strange woman behind the Cracker Barrel. Now, I'm not embarrassed to admit it's been a while since I've been with a woman. After Constance, I just haven't had it in me to date much, but the way Tallulah kissed was unlike anything I've ever experienced. It wasn't awkward at all and in fact felt more natural and passionate than kissing any woman I have ever been with. I'll spare you the

43

details, Mom, but I got so caught up in it that my hands began caressing her body and she didn't seem to mind. I won't tell you the thoughts that followed.

For that short time, I wouldn't necessarily say I was happy because I'm not sure I remember what happiness feels like exactly, but I wasn't unhappy. It was amazing to me that someone I just met a short time earlier could manage to temporarily lift the storm clouds from my head, although there really were storm clouds everywhere. At least those had nothing to do with how I felt inside.

Now this is the part that scares the shit out of me. This is what I was dreading to write about because during the one hour of sleep I was able to get last night, this part of yesterday haunted every second of it. I don't remember having such vicious, nerve shattering nightmares in my whole life. I wish it wasn't real, but I like to think that I'm only depressed--not crazy--and I know what I saw. What I wish I didn't see. Okay, I'll try my best to be thorough. I'm so frightened that I feel like my brain is already trying to repress these unwanted memories.

The rain was coming down heavier than ever and the lightning crashes were getting louder but Tallulah and I didn't seem to care. Then I thought I heard someone saying something and looked over to my right for a second. Standing a few feet away, there were two men watching us. One was middle-aged, with balding brown hair and a beard. He was slightly overweight and a little shorter than me.

What I noticed most about him though were his eyes. They were dark--black even--and had the most incredible look of vacancy imaginable. These were empty, soulless eyes. There was only one other place I had ever seen eyes like this and that was at work. His eyes resembled those of a typical cadaver at the funeral home. Now that I think of it, there have been some dead people before me with more life and compassion in their eyes than this man. No matter where I look I can't keep from seeing those eyes staring right through me.

The other guy with him was much younger—twenty, maybe. I couldn't really tell. He was about my height and build but thinner. It was hard to completely make out his face because he had dark shoulder length hair which concealed most of it. Somehow, his eyes were also prominent, despite the unseen face. They were the same as his friend's. Only his were more scrutinizing with a touch of malice. They scared me even more. He might have been smiling, wickedly, behind the hair and rain.

Tallulah finally noticed them too and asked rather sarcastically if they saw something they liked? The older one smiled which made my blood run cold. He said very calmly, "Are you two having a good time?" Fear disabled my ability to speak so Tallulah replied with a "We were until a couple of creepy perverts came along." The older one smiled even bigger now and turned to look at his friend, who was indeed smiling too under all that long, wet hair. I was on the verge of nervous hyper-ventilation now. That's when I noticed the older one was brandishing a large hunting knife. If it were any longer it could be considered a short sword. When I focused my eyes better I could see it had dried blood on it. I imagined it wasn't from a deer.

His young friend then retrieved a cruel looking knife from his back pocket. It looked like something used for human sacrifices where the end

45

result is the releasing of ancient demons upon the Earth. I've never been stabbed before and I'm sure it hurts regardless of the knife but this particular knife looked like it would hurt the most. I didn't know if I was more scared of the knife or the person who would carry such a thing.

The older one took a step forward, running his eyes up and down Tallulah, while disgustingly licking his lips. Still smiling, he said, "We wanna have a good time too." If there is a single brave bone in my body then it's broken because I could not move or breathe after that. Tallulah wasn't fazed though. She moved closer to the older knife wielding man, burning with anger. "You think I'm scared of you fuck-faces? You think you're the only people with knives around here?" Even more surprising to me than her outburst, Tallulah reached into her purse and pulled out an equally dangerous looking knife. What the fuck is going on, I thought.

She began waving her knife around, shouting obscenities, which both men giggled at. I swear, if their smiles alone frightened me into paralysis, their malevolent laughter almost emptied my bladder where I stood.

The older one crept closer and told Tallulah, "Stop waving around that knife, you little bitch, or someone's gonna get hurt." "Yeah. You!" she immediately shouted back. From her bold response, I was starting to feel something else mixing with my fear and cowardice--it was shame kicking in big time. I mean, I think the average person would have been scared too but Tallulah wasn't. It was as if she's fought her way out of this situation numerous times.

The younger one spoke in a raspy, deep tone that reminded me of a villain in some 1980s horror movie. It sounded like a ghoul was trying to come across as human as possible in order to fool someone but couldn't quite get it right. He said, "If you give us the knife, we'll kill you second...after we have a little fun with you first, of course." Both men giggled again. This was getting worse by the millisecond.

The older one locked eyes with Tallulah and told his partner, "I don't think this lousy little cunt wants to have any fun. Well that's too bad, because I'll be honest, there's nothing like sodomy in the rain. Now give me that fuckin' thing!"

The older guy suddenly lunged for Tallulah's arm, but she was able to avoid him. As if second nature to her, Tallulah took a quick swipe at the man with her blade. A dark red line instantly took form along his neck and then came forth a tremendous gushing of blood. I know it was just a few seconds, but it felt like hours as I stood there, clinging helplessly to the wall, as the life poured out of this man's neck in a thick, crimson mess. I can't even describe how terrible it was to see that. If it weren't for what followed, that image would be the worst of my nightmares for as long as I live.

As the older man fell dead to the floor, the younger one sprung forward with an animal quality, his knife raised. In my terror, I was completely useless and had to watch as the long haired attacker got the better of Tallulah. His cruel looking blade came down hard and buried itself in her chest. She let out a gasp of pain I will never, ever forget even if lost my mind to dementia or Alzheimer's. Her eyes went wide and she turned her head slightly to look at me. I wish she hadn't. Oh God, I wish she hadn't looked at me at that moment.

47

The younger man then started repeatedly stabbing her abdomen in a rapid motion. He must have stabbed her at least a dozen times. The sick fuck then gave her a big sloppy kiss as she died. The blood that had gushed out of her mouth was all over his. A few minutes ago I was kissing those same lips of hers. I was caressing her wonderful body. Now both are covered in blood, dead and gone. Just like that. A few minutes ago there was a light at the end of my never-ending tunnel. Dim as it may have been, it was still a light. If I lived in a shadow before, it was nothing compared to the darkness that engulfed me now.

Almost without thinking I bent down to pick up Tallulah's knife at my feet. My hand was shaking so bad it's a wonder I could hold it at all. I backed up a little as the long haired ghoul peered down at his dead friend. He then noticed I was still standing there and charged at me with an awful roar. I instantly blacked out for what I imagine was no more than a second or two. A sudden surge of white hot pain took over me during those lost moments. As it faded and I regained focus, my worst fear was confirmed. The younger attacker was standing before me, his stare locked onto my face. The malice in his horrid eyes was gone. They were now as empty as his friend's. He let out a soft gasp and appeared dizzy all of sudden. It wasn't until further investigation did I realize why. Tallulah's knife, which I was still clutching tightly, was piercing his chest all of the way up to the handle. There was no doubt the blade had just ripped through his heart.

I couldn't move an inch. Even a single blink was not feasible at that moment. I just stood there, quietly, not really sure what I was thinking. Without speaking, the young ghoul softly pushed himself away from me,

48

forcing the blade to dislodge. He remained on his feet momentarily then collapsed next to Tallulah's body. Dead.

I'm sure my catatonia didn't actually last as long as it felt in my mind but when I finally realized what had just taken place and what I'd done, I threw up what felt like everything I've ever eaten in my entire life. I knew my actions were justifiable self-defense but that didn't make taking a life any easier. I work with dead people all day, but I don't kill them first. Despite his wicked intentions, when it sunk in that the long haired psychopath at my feet was dead and I had made that so, I was overcome with a dreadful feeling of sinking within myself and I couldn't stop it. It felt like I was falling through a dark abyss and I knew I would eventually fall to my death but couldn't see the ground so I never knew when it was coming exactly.

So I just kind of stood there looking at the three bloody bodies on the ground. There was now a good deal of red in the rain water that flowed into the nearby drain. I had absolutely no idea what to do next. Call the police perhaps. Go back inside the Cracker Barrel and get help. Take off in my car and never look back. I just didn't know where to begin.

That's when it happened--the most frightening, unexplainable, unimaginable thing I have ever experienced. I know it was real, but I've been praying ever since that it was just a dream. A terrifying, extremely detailed nightmare that could never intrude on my waking life. I can see it happening in my mind over and over and I can't make it stop.

Lying dead in puddles of blood and rain, Tallulah and the two men slowly sat up. They all turned their faces towards me, as I'm sure they've never

49

seen a more mortified person as I was. The three of them smiled. Smiled! Tallulah then said something to the effect of, "What's the matter, Guy? Never had one of them sit up on you at work?" I don't remember fainting, but I know I did.

I must have been out for hours since it was now dark outside. As I awoke, I instantly felt constricted and uncomfortable. I forced my eyes open and the first thing I saw was my reflection in a ceiling mirror. I was dressed in a suit and lying in a coffin with a white rose in my hand. I don't need to tell you that I panicked. I couldn't believe I was dead. I didn't want to be dead. Was this the same funeral home I worked at? I sat up as quickly as I could, which was a mistake because I felt the room start to spin. I could feel a bandage on the back of my head. I must have hit it on the ground when I fainted. It stung. If I felt pain though, that meant I wasn't dead. And as soon as the room stopped moving, I realized I wasn't in a funeral home, but someone's house.

On the nightstand I noticed the same coffin-shaped purse that Tallulah was carrying. I'm guessing it was her bedroom I was in. It looked liked someplace Bela Lugosi would find cozy. It was creepy and very gothic with lots of purple and black; enough candles to put Bath & Body Works to shame. This bedroom was the arch enemy of sunshine. It was actually more of a crypt than a bedroom.

I slowly, and painfully, lifted myself out of the coffin and stood next to it. My suit was coming off as I moved around. It was the type of suit we use sometimes at work for bodies that are to be viewed at a service but the family has asked us to provide the clothing. They're cut up the middle in the back. That makes it easier to dress the body for placement in the casket. I didn't like that I was dressed like this. It really gave me the heebie jeebies so I took the suit off right away. I'm glad whoever put me in it left my regular clothes on underneath.

Somewhere in the house I could faintly hear the sound of music. There was a choir singing in a very haunting manner. It could only be a requiem or something of that nature. Under normal circumstances I might have actually liked this piece of music, but I was too busy being confused and scared to enjoy it. Of course, at this time I was under the impression that I had not really seen what I thought I saw. People didn't rise from the dead after being stabbed repeatedly or having their throats slit. I love a good zombie movie as much as the next person but things like that just didn't happen in real life. Dead was dead. I knew that better than most people. So I must have hallucinated. Or perhaps I fainted after stabbing that guy and puking and the three of them getting up to smile at me was all in my head. Although, that didn't explain how I had gotten to the house. Who brought me there?

I inched my way out of the spooky bedroom, trying not to make a sound. I found myself in a barely lit hallway with several doors and a descending staircase. The music seemed to be coming from downstairs and I wanted to get the hell out of there so I carefully tip-toed down the stairs. The music got louder with each step.

When I got to the bottom I lost my breath. Sitting in the living room opposite me was Tallulah and the two men that attacked us. The younger one who I stabbed was in a love seat, clumsily trying to light a cigarette with no luck. I thought he was either drunk off his ass or completely wasted on drugs. He paid no mind to me at all.

The older guy was looking right at me--again with a smile. He sat on a couch next to Tallulah who was also smiling at me. They both had glasses of wine in their hands. There was at least three empty bottles around them and a multitude of pills on the coffee table. I recognized some of them from my own prescriptions. Mostly sleeping pills and anti-depressants. I had no idea what was going on. Every part of me felt like high-tailing it out of there at warp speed. I wanted to just run and run until every vein in my body exploded. But I was as good as nailed to the spot I stood. I couldn't see my face but I'm sure it was pale and wide-eyed.

These people were supposed to be dead. I saw each of them die. No one survives what happened to them and even by some remote chance they hung on, the last thing they'd be doing right now is hanging out at home, getting blasted. They'd be in the hospital, clinging to life; hooked up to machines or at least some sort of medical apparatus. But here they were, seemingly alive. Aside from their current intoxicated nature, there didn't seem to be anything wrong with them. Even the older guy's throat looked exactly how it did before Tallulah slashed it. Were they ghosts? That would make more sense. That I could believe easier. It would still terrify me but I'd rather be scared than crazy.

Tallulah poured herself more wine and then made it a point to inform me that it was kind of cute when I freaked out the way I did. The way I was still freaking out.

I managed to ask them what they were doing. It's the only words I could put together. The older man told me that they were just practicing. For what, was beyond me. He said that they had downed a ton of miscellaneous pills with several bottles of wine. Tallulah asked me, "How do you think I should position myself for when the police find me?" What! She went on to inquire, "Should I die in here with these knuckleheads or in the bathroom? Personally, I think its way sexier to die in the kitchen. Don't you agree?"

I was trembling inside but if this was some sort of sick joke I didn't find it amusing at all. I demanded some answers. The younger guy fell out of his seat, hitting the floor hard. He looked dead again. His cigarette, still stuck to his lips, went unlit.

I recounted what I could remember about the incident outside the Cracker Barrel leading up to the coffin and crashing their little drinking/pill popping party. Tallulah actually seemed a bit disappointed at my mood. She tried to justify some of what happened. "You didn't like the coffin? I thought it was a nice touch. I figured I'd give you a little taste of what you usually provide. You know, to get a feel for being dead." I didn't like it. I can think of very few things I disliked more.

The older guy was losing his composure rapidly from the booze and sedatives. From what I could understand through his slurred words I think he said, "But you said you wanted to die. We're just trying to help you out." No more than a second after this statement, he fell forward with a loud crash as his head smashed into the coffee table, sending pills and wine bottles everywhere. He looked dead as well.

I told Tallulah that I didn't understand any of this. All I knew was that I saw three people die that day and now they were before me and appeared to be dying all over again. It made no sense and I wanted nothing to do with it. If I was going to die, it would be on my watch.

My way.

She managed to smile again, although it probably took all of her strength. Her eyes were starting to roll back when she spoke again. She sounded like a tape player whose batteries were losing power. "Speaking of dying, the pills and wine are really kicking in now. If this doesn't work, we can continue this conversation in the morning." A couple of seconds later her head dropped back and she wasn't breathing.

I had to know if this was real or if I was stuck in some elaborate hidden camera show. I cautiously made my way over to Tallulah and put my ear to her chest. No heartbeat. I felt for a pulse and didn't find one. She was dead. I was sure of that. Now instead of standing amongst three brutally murdered and bloodied dead bodies, I was standing amongst three overdosed dead bodies. My situation had improved very little, if at all.

Before I had the chance to really start turning into a fucking basket case I spotted my car keys on the coffee table, amongst whatever pills the older guy hadn't knocked off with his unintentional head butt. I grabbed them and ran for the front door. The lightning and thunder had let up but it was still raining pretty steadily. My car was parked outside, just behind a Black 1971 Plymouth Barracuda. I recognized that car right away because I always wanted one as a kid. I didn't hang around to ogle it, but whichever of the three it belonged to, I could easily tell they took good care of it. It made my car look like crap.

Nevertheless, I jumped into my crappy car and got the fuck out of there. I was careful to not take off too drastically. The last thing I wanted was some cop to pull me over for speeding. Knowing me, I'd start telling them all about what happened without realizing it and I'd end up in jail or some fucking nut house where I'd never be able to kill myself because I'd either be too doped up or they'd take away my belt and shoelaces forever.

I was so jittery all the way home. I probably looked like one of those stupid cartoon characters where the animation kind of vibrates, even when someone is standing still. I don't know. Never mind. I don't know what the fuck I'm talking about.

You were probably still out with your friends when I got home, Bruno, so you didn't see how distraught I was. It didn't help that it was only after I threw myself onto my bed that I noticed one of your dogs had taken a big shit on it.

After cleaning up, I laid there and I cried and cried and cried. I threw up a couple of times too, replaying the day's events. It wasn't until I decided to write this letter (which has become a small novel) did I finally get up and move to the corner of the room where I'm sitting now.

I can't do this. There is no way. How I can possibly continue to live my life knowing these people are out there? Knowing what I did? Even if they appeared to have come back to life, I know I killed someone. And I know I saw two other people die before me. I don't care how elaborate a prank can be, it was real. And besides, I'd have to be in on it in some way to carry out

55

my end. But then who would the prank be on if I was part of it? If it was a prank on me, then it went horribly wrong because the knife I picked up was real and I really did stab a man in the heart with it. Yet, somehow, hours later, there he is, sitting in a recliner, trying to light a cigarette while fucked up.

I can't begin to think what the fuck these three people might be. My mind is racing with thoughts of every horror movie or novel I've ever read and the possibilities aren't only endless, they ALL scare the living shit out of me. I simply cannot live, knowing such things exist.

I wanted to die before because I was sad. I'm still sad. Immensely sad, but now I'm also filled with dread. That isn't altogether new. I always dreaded many things throughout my day from dealing with Bruno's assortment of pets and pies to running into Constance, but this dread is unlike any I've ever felt. It's like the type of dread a child probably feels when his abusive, alcoholic father comes home and the child suddenly remembers he left a bunch of toys on the floor by the front door. The type of dread someone feels when they're waiting for test results from their doctor and they just know the news will be bad. The type of dread an innocent man on Death Row feels the night before their execution.

The way I feel it's a wonder I haven't died already from stress. I felt bad before. Now, I'm the very person the word "misery" was created for. I'm someone's failed marriage. I'm a malignant tumor in some kid's head. I'm a dead Grandmother by the fireplace on Christmas Day. I'm footage of your dearest loved one getting beheaded by kidnappers while they're still conscious.

THE FUNERAL PORTRAIT

It's not a matter anymore of me wanting to die. I know now that I must die. There is absolutely no fucking way I can go on now. I cannot be reached at this point. All the positivity in the world can't alter the negativity of my existence. Everyone knows when you combine the two you'll always end up with a negative. So I see it only fitting that I subtract myself from your lives—from this whole fucking awful mess you call living.

I love you all so very much. I haven't much love to give but believe me when I say the little that is there is all yours. Please remember me for any good times we might have had, and not for my fate.

Goodbye.

Guy

APRIL 21ST

To My Dear Parents,

It has been a week since my run in with that Tallulah woman and her two, I guess you can say friends, but who knows for sure. I'm a bit less on edge than I was directly after it happened but that isn't saying much. I took a couple of days off from work to get my head together as much as I could. I wanted to take the whole week but Mr. Bates said we were too busy. Sometimes I don't know why he bothered hiring Devlin. He's supposed to fill my shoes when I'm not there but Mr. Bates seems to think I'm the only person in the world who can get a body ready for viewing. It's really annoying.

I noticed he's been making me work more ever since Devlin screwed up the Rittenhouse funeral. I don't remember if I told you about that. We had a job involving this old guy that lived in the same community as my friend, Mr. Friar. Devlin, in his stupid attempt to prove he could prepare a body faster than me, forgot to secure Rittenhouse's mouth shut. So during the service when one of his grandchildren leaned over to kiss his forehead, Rittenhouse's mouth opened ever so slightly. Several people fainted, other's cried harder than they already were crying and a couple of mourners became catatonic.

That wasn't as horrific as the three dead bodies I saw rising up but the average person doesn't react well to their dead loved ones showing any signs

58

of life at their own funeral, no matter how subtle. Mr. Bates was furious and would've canned Devlin if I didn't vouch for him. I made up something about it being my fault because I distracted Devlin or something like that. I could care less about Devlin, but I didn't want to get stuck with his workload. I guess I got it anyway. Mr. Bates barely lets Devlin vacuum without watching him.

God, I hate saying "Mr. Bates". It sounds too close to masturbates. I don't know why he doesn't just go by his first name, Philip. I can't help but shake my head whenever a client or mourners enter the funeral home and he says, Hello, I'm Mr. Bates. It sounds like he's saying, Hello, I masturbate. Every now and then you can kind of notice a small reaction from people as they take a second to think of what they might have heard and what he actually said. Hello, I'm Philip Bates. That approach is simple, effective and with much less chance of being misunderstood as the unwanted confession of a goddamn perverted degenerate. No one wants to leave their expired loved ones with a chronic masturbator. All the wrong thoughts will be going through their heads during the service when they should be focusing on mourning.

So I've tried to block out what happened the other day as often as possible, but often isn't often enough for my liking. Sometimes I wish we were like computers and we could just delete memories as if they were diseased files that wreaked havoc on our internal hard drives. Then again, if I could do that I probably wouldn't be the way I am in the first place.

I was trying to sleep late on one of the days I took off but was awakened by a monster of a St. Bernard licking my face. As I got up, Bruno was standing by my bedroom door laughing. He's my brother and I love him, but Mom, I'm convinced it was Satan who knocked you up all those years ago, while Dad was mowing the lawn or something.

The dog barked and I jumped back, sort of hiding behind my comforter. "It's just a dog, you big pussy" was what I got for that move. That thing was more like Cujo though. It looked like a float in the Halloween Parade. And apparently, the beast was sick so Bruno brought it home from the pet store. He told me--told, not asked--to walk him a couple of times during the day while he was at work. Before I could protest, Bruno slammed my door closed and was gone. Of course the hell hound started growling. Great.

I decided I would try to make the best of the situation so I put the dog in my car, which was no easy task, and drove over to Constance's job. Yeah, I know, that doesn't sound like making the best of anything. I took a chance.

Constance now works at the Chili's next to that small movie theater whose slushy machines never work. I don't even know why they have those. Even more so I don't know why I insist on ordering one whenever I go there only to be told the machines are out of order. I wish they'd get rid of them. It's like those stupid gas station convenience stores that have public restroom signs and then you stop in, ready to piss your pants and they tell you the toilet is busted. But, hey, at least their slushy machines are usually in working order.

So I pulled around back of the Chili's and wouldn't you know it, there was Constance sitting on the curb, having a cigarette. She told me she had quit smoking last time we spoke. I guess it didn't take. That or she was lying. Probably the latter.

I made sure she didn't see me parking and quietly got out of my car. The yeti dog I was watching for Bruno decided it could make enough noise for the both of us. I'm going to be wiping drool off of my dashboard for weeks. After struggling with this stupid dog, if it was in fact a dog and not the missing link, I closed the passenger side door and turned around to face Constance who was now staring at me.

"Guy?" I was tempted to say no and jump back in the car or at least take off, riding on the dog (yes, it would have definitely supported my weight) but I knew it was a rhetorical question. The best I could do was to pretend I had no idea she'd be there at that moment.

"What are you doing here?" I could already detect a stern tone in her voice. That was always the first phase of the cruelty she could unleash if provoked. Like an idiot, the first thing that came to my lips was the old "I was just in the neighborhood" shpeal. She didn't buy it, given that both my home and job are miles away, I prefer Applebee's to Chili's and I couldn't possibly be taking in a movie accompanied by a dog--even if this one could pass for a rather large, hairy woman.

I tried, as casually and friendly as possible, to tell her that I had to watch the dog for Bruno and I was taking him for a walk. "Then why aren't you walking?" I actually love this woman?

I informed Constance that I was taking the dog to the park, which was true. She immediately pointed out that I overshot the park by about three miles. She was entering phase two. I asked her what was wrong. I wasn't doing anything. "You know what you're doing, Guy?" I froze and simply muttered,

"What?" It was barely a whisper but she had caught it and I'll never forget the rest of this interaction:

"Jesus! Why can't you just leave me alone? I tried, all right? I tried so hard but that's it! I'm fed up!"

I don't understand.

"You fucking understand. You're just too stubborn to let it register in that goddamn twisted head of yours."

Hey, there's no need for that language. It's ugly.

"Well then fuck-fuck-fucking-fuck, okay?! This is me being fucking ugly. Isn't this a big turn-off? Don't you just want to turn around and run away and leave the foul-mouthed ugly girl the fuck alone?"

Why are you doing this?

"Because you don't listen! Every week you come by here and I have to try my best to be civil with you. I can't take it anymore. What we had is done so fucking get over it. I'm trying to get on with my life, Guy. You should do the same."

I couldn't even respond. I had so much anger and contempt in me at that moment that my mouth was sealed shut. I won't even share with you the thoughts that raced through my head. She demanded to know if I was even listening to her. I just bit my lip as hard as I could. It wasn't long before I could taste my own blood in my mouth.

"That's fucking it! If you come here again I'm calling the police. You fucking lunatic."

And without a word from me, she stomped her way back to work. The anger I felt was like an axe to the head. That particular anger was short-lived though because it was replaced by an entirely new anger when a stray cat suddenly scurried by, prompting Bruno's hell hound to chase it.

Of course I was holding its leash securely and it very easily dragged me across the back parking lot and face first into a shitload of garbage. Chili's garbage.

My only solace was the thought I might get accidentally tossed into a compactor with the rest of the trash. Instead, I drove home smelling like rotting food. Plus, I forgot to actually walk the dog and given its size you better believe the magnitude of the shit he took in my backseat was unbelievable. I'll probably set my car on fire.

Frustrated,

Guy

APRIL 23RD

To My Dear Family,

As you can imagine, going to see Constance and what went down with her didn't do much to relax my nerves. Nothing does. The one thing that will relax them permanently stresses me out more because I can't get up the courage to just go for it. Sometimes I wish dying was as easy as picking out a pair of sneakers.

Who am I kidding? I take such a long time trying to pick out sneakers sometimes that I end up just going home without anything. If dying were based on the ability to make one's mind up in a timely fashion I'd live for thousands of years. Why no, Miss, I'm not a vampire but I do suck the life out of people. And I bet you I'd put up with that shit too. Immortality, I mean. Eons would go by and there'd be nothing left of the Earth but little ol' stupid me, floating around space where the planet used to be, sighing heavily for all eternity at the thought that all life has ended, yet I go on. Sigh.

I barely slept last night because every time I closed my eyes all I could see was that Tallulah woman. She was covered in blood from head to toe. Only the whites of her eyes provided any color other than red. Even her pupils were a deep crimson, kind of like when you take a picture and the lack of a red-eye reduction option on the camera makes everyone look like demons.

After awhile I would notice that she wasn't just covered in blood, she was completely burned. Her skin was black and charred. I could smell the burnt flesh and it was awful. I even began gagging a couple of times because I was sure I could smell it. I could almost feel the heat from her, as if she were engulfed in a ball of invisible fire that you couldn't see but burned you just the same.

She moved towards me at such a slow pace it was as if she wasn't moving all. And although she looked far away, it felt like her outstretched hand was a mere inch or two from my face. I tried to run away but the young crazy looking man was holding me by the wrist. I tried everything to break free, but he had a death-grip on me. I punched his face, I clawed at it, even creating gashes in it somehow but he would only laugh the more I fought him. Never did his hand loosen in the slightest way from the hold he had on me. The older guy was there too. He sat on the ground nearby and was crying hysterically while stabbing himself repeatedly. It looked like he was punishing himself for something I couldn't understand. Stab after stab he would burst into tears, occasionally letting loose this horrible scream, only to cut himself off by slashing his own throat.

They were the most terrifying images I had ever seen and no matter where I looked, I could see all three at the same time playing in my head. A triple feature of fucked up horrific shit all showing on a single screen simultaneously. I woke up so scared several times I was sure it was just a matter of time before I died of cardiac arrest. No such luck though. Instead, I continued to see this nightmare go on and on, until after maybe thirty minutes of sleep total, I decided to give up on sleeping altogether. I'm running on fumes right now. My goal is to just pass out without warning. That way I'd be too tired to bother waking up. Hopefully, I'll be too tired to even dream.

What gets me even more pissed off is that I went to see Dr. Petersen yesterday in an effort to handle my problems in a more adult manner and this is my reward? Instead of shrinking my head, he fills it with scary thoughts, is that how it works? I'd rather accidentally stumble upon Leatherface's house than have nightmares like that again.

I know it's not really the doctor's fault. It's just upsetting to pay for a psychiatrist and then feel worse afterwards. I already feel bad as it is that you're the one who actually pays for the sessions Dad. I appreciate it though. I try to make progress so you don't feel like you're throwing your money away. But I like to work out as many of my problems as I can on my own first. You probably think I should be in Dr. Petersen's office twenty-four hours a day by that assessment.

I do want to get better, that's the truth. It's not always easy to make progress with Dr. Petersen. I hate his office. It's so stale with all its grays and browns. When I lie on his couch most of the time I can't even concentrate because I'm paranoid his stupid wall-mounted shelf full of books is going to fall on me. Why would he put it there of all places? Does he even need that stupid bookshelf packed with over-sized editions of unreadable books? I get it, he's smarter than me. A simple degree hanging on the wall will do. Oh, wait, he has that too. Three of them! What a pompous ass. And how is someone supposed to feel better when his walls are the color of angry storm clouds, hovering over you, ready to rain on your parade? I'm sure I'm just reading into things and making way too much of all this. I'm sorry.

66

Anyways, I went to see him and he thought my sudden need for a session was due to you starting up the whole pie throwing thing again, Bruno. Surprisingly, you haven't been tossing any baked goods at me the past week. I'm guessing it's that diet you're trying to stick to. Doesn't help to have pies hanging around when you're trying to lose weight.

I knew the doctor would be mad at me when I told him my real reason for seeking him out. He promised he wouldn't get angry because it's not his business too. "Oh, I have been disappointed in you on occasion but never angry. Please, give me more credit than that." That's what he said. Of course when I told him I had went to see Constance twice he flipped the fuck out. This is what that lying old bastard had to say, "How could you do something so stupid? What in God's name do you think you're coming here for? To forget about that evil woman! Then after all of our progress you go and see her behind my back? Ooh, that makes me so ang--"

I know what that asshole was going to say but he changed it quick to "disappointed." He was very "disappointed" with me. I had to tell him why I decided to go see Constance but to be honest I didn't really know. I guess I just wanted to see her. Luckily the good doctor calmed down and asked me what happened when I went to her job. I told him about how she got bitchy with me and starting screaming at me, saying horrible, hurtful things.

I also told him how I didn't react like I normally did (putting my head down and fighting back tears.) I told him how the whole time she was yelling at me all I could imagine is how her facial expression would change if I just suddenly reached out and starting choking her. I thought, "She'd be nice to me then because she would want something from me again. She would want me to stop. She'd need me to stop. I'd be needed by her in some way. It's not really what I would want her to want from me but it'd be something right?" Fuck. I hadn't planned on telling you what I was thinking at that moment. Oh well, now that I've written it, you probably should know exactly how fucking deranged I've become.

Dr. Petersen certainly seemed to be disturbed by my account of the situation. He scolded me for some time saying things like "What's happening to you, Guy?" and "Where is this kind of thinking coming from?" I wasn't going to do it, you know. It was just a thought. A random, senseless, meaningless thought. I know getting rid of Constance isn't the solution to my problems. I don't know what came over me then. I'm sorry if it scared you. It won't happen again.

Dickhead Petersen then gave me a lecture on how if I did something like that to Constance then he failed to do his job and he couldn't be much help to me from behind a pane of prison glass and bullshit, bullshit, bullshit. After he was sure I felt like an absolutely worthless bag of pterodactyl shit, he pressed me for info on the previous time I had went to go see Constance. I didn't tell you guys about that for some reason. I think I might have been too upset to write it down. I didn't want to tell Petersen either. I told him that he'd be angry at me. He said, "I think we've opened that door already, so why don't you just come on out and say what you need to." Do people actually ever get better from seeing therapists?

What happened the previous time I went to go see Constance was that she treated me very nicely. From beginning to end it was a pleasant experience. But as I drove home I started to think about our interaction and it began to dawn on me that she wasn't actually being pleasant--she was being indifferent. And that hurt more than anything.

I would rather her hate me than to feel absolutely nothing for me. I can't imagine any of you know what it feels like to have been close to someone the way her and I were and to know if I died today she would feel absolutely nothing. She wouldn't be sad. She wouldn't be happy. She just wouldn't care. God, that fucking hurts like you wouldn't believe. Real physical pain in addition to the mental agony.

Even people you might have been involved with for the briefest period of time, whether it be a friend, a co-worker, a lover--even they would at least feel bad to hear of your passing. With Constance, I'm guaranteed not an ounce of emotion. I'm like some dull television show she's seen a few times but never really got into. If it stays on the air, that's fine. If it gets canceled, no big deal. Life continues as normal. To know you have no meaning to someone that means so much to you is more than anyone should be asked to handle.

Petersen said he wasn't angry but I knew he was lying because he snapped his pencil in half when I told him my way of dealing with that meeting was going to the roof of the factory. Initially, I tried to be creative in battling my gloom and went to the mall to see whatever comedy had just opened that Friday. This was the same day I saw Constance shopping for clothes with one of her friends, having the time of her life like her indifference didn't just shred my heart to bloody shards the day before. I couldn't get over her carefree demeanor and so like I was trying to avoid, I ended up on the roof again.

If you remember, this was also the day that I met Tallulah and those other men. When Dr. Petersen asked me what stopped me from jumping off the roof, I told him that I had met a woman. I didn't mention the note I had found there before but I explained to him how I couldn't jump because Tallulah kept bugging me for a light and eventually pushed me. Not the most conventional method but it did scare me enough to climb back up and get off the roof. Then I told the doctor how she and I actually clicked over lunch but things got, for lack of a better term, strange. I left it at that. I thought I had proved my insanity enough for one day.

I was shocked the fart face maggot didn't push me to keep talking. He did make it a point though to further elaborate on how disappointed he was in how I've been handling myself. He gave me a new, stronger, prescription and made me promise to be back in his office next week. As he wrote it out, I suddenly became aware again of how stuffy it was in that office and asked if I could open a window. I must have been sporting one hell of a sourpuss because he refused to open the window and asked me to move away from it. Jumping out of his window wasn't even on my mind, but after he alluded to it, I thought it would be pretty funny to fling myself from his 5th floor office. Good luck getting patients after something like that, you dickless King of Lies. I really hate psychiatrists, Dad, I'm sorry. I just don't think they're honest. Sometimes I think people become crazy only after being "treated" by them.

I didn't get that prescription filled. I guess I should go do that now. I love you all. Please don't think I don't appreciate your help, even if I feel helpless.

THE FUNERAL PORTRAIT

Best Wishes From Loserville,

Guy

APRIL 24TH

To My Dear Family,

Yesterday I went to fill my prescription from Dr. Petersen and I was thinking about everything he said, plus what happened with Constance and I was certain I would throw myself off the roof of that factory once and for all. When I got there though, all I did was stand on the edge, crying. I don't care so much about what Dr. Petersen thinks but I thought about what a disappointment I must be to you. You probably never thought the smiling little baby you brought into the world would turn into such a mess. You probably wonder on a daily basis what you did wrong. I hope you know you didn't do anything wrong. I'm just damaged goods, missing the necessary components to function on a level consistent with typical happiness or at least in a relative state of complacency. Unfortunately, I'm yours. Like a spur of the moment tattoo that was clearly a mistake. You're stuck.

It was starting to drizzle and I thought I'd better just suck it up for another day and head home when someone said, "Right back where you started, huh?" It was her. I should have known. I did my best to look extremely annoyed in order to mask my fear. I guess she bought it because she said sarcastically, "It's nice to see you too, Guy." I couldn't deal with this again, whatever it was so I asked, "Why don't you get out of here?" She didn't budge though. She said she wanted to make a deal. I just wanted to be left alone--most of all by her. She said, unfazed, "Oh, don't be that way. Life's more fun when you play along." I reminded her that life sucks. She suddenly agreed with me and told me to "scoot over" so she could stand on the outer side of the railing where I was. What the hell was she doing?

"What the hell are you doing?" I asked. The same as me apparently since I was ending it all. Then she started asking how I wanted to do this? Did I want her to go first or did I want to jump at the same time? "What works for you, Guy?" she asked so casually as if inquiring whether I wanted cake with my tea. Do people eat cake with tea? Or is it only with those stupid biscuit things that are really just cookies?

I asked her, "Why do you keep bothering me?" She said she thought she could help me. Exactly how she could do that, I had not one possible clue. Tallulah figured based on the sort of person I was, kind but depressed and weak, that she could give me incentive to go through with my suicide. That incentive, she informed me, was guilt.

I didn't understand. How could I, when everything that came out of her mouth had this twinge of mystery to it like her words had endless volumes of hidden meanings to them? Instead I stared at her in silence, still trying to look annoyed, in the hopes she would elaborate. Before she would explain though she put a cigarette in between her lips and wanted to know if I was still carrying my "cute little lighter." I always do. Now, I was genuinely annoyed as I lit her cigarette.

"Thanks. As I was saying, guilt is the key. If I can get you to kill me, maybe the guilt of taking a life will force you to finally take your own. What do you think of that, Guy?"

Were the marbles falling out of my fucking head as we spoke? What the hell was she talking about? "Maybe you haven't noticed, Tallulah, whatever your name is, but I could have sworn I took a life already." She smiled. It was a warm smile. I enjoyed it more than I'd like to admit. "You did," she said, still smiling. On top of that I saw her get killed as well so why wasn't she dead?

"I can't die." Her words were now somber and the smile was gone. Looking at her expression then, if I hadn't seen her smile already, I would've thought her face had never experienced so much as a grin. Maybe the marbles are falling out of both our heads. I asked her why she couldn't die.

"I don't know why. I just can't. I want to. I've been trying for some time now but it never sticks. No matter what I do to myself I always wake up in the end as if it never happened." So you really can't die? At all? "No. I really can't." How is that possible? "Like I said, I don't know what caused it but I'm not the only one. Gus and Kovac--they can't die either."

Gus and Kovac? Are those the two freaks you were with? "Yes. They're in the same boat as me. They want to die too but they can't. None of us can explain it." So, and I'm just going to pretend for a second like this isn't some fucked up dream caused by my meds, you and your buddies are immortal, but you don't want to be. "Basically. Yes." Are you vampires--because as long as I'm pretending to believe in people who can't die, I might as well believe in

74

vampires too. "No, we're not vampires, silly." You're just incapable of dying for some unknown reason and you want me to figure out how to put an end to that? "Yes."

Are you crazy? Do you realize how many people would love to live forever? "I could care less about living forever. Do you want to live forever?" No--actually--I don't. "Do you even want to live through tonight?" No--I don't. "Right. Well neither do I. This isn't a gift. It's a curse, Guy. I'm cursed with immortality. I don't want this life anymore than you want yours."

Why me? Why do you think I can help you?

"We thought you might have been like us but you're not. You took a nasty bruise to the back of your head that hung around for awhile. For us, that would have cleared up in minutes." It hurt for days. I couldn't even wear a hat. I mean, I don't wear hats much but I tried to put one on and it hurt. "You see? You're not like us at all. You want to die just as much as we do, only you have the means and we have the motivation. I thought it'd make sense for us to help each other out. I know you're a nice guy and I know if you really did kill us, you're the kind of person that just couldn't live with that on your conscience."

All right, I think I have everything in order here. You and your buddies can't die but you want to and you think if I figure out a way to make that happen I'll be so consumed with guilt that I'll be inspired to finally carry out my own death. That's your offer? "Pretty much. You kill us, feel terrible about it and then kill yourself. Everyone is happy. Criss-cross."

I told her goodbye and tried to climb back over the railing but she stopped me by clutching my arm. Like her smile, I enjoyed the embrace but wouldn't show her that. She just grabbed my arm, no big deal, but there was this sort of intimacy about it I can't explain.

"I'm being totally serious, Guy. You've seen it with your own eyes. We can't die. We need your help." I didn't know what to think. "Oh, come on. Is your life getting any better?" No. In fact it was worse since I last saw her. "See?"

She was holding my hand now. It felt so nice. "Do you remember when we kissed that day behind the restaurant, Guy?" How could I forget? None of my hats that I never wear fit me. "Did you like kissing me?" I did until I was forced to commit what I thought at the time was murder. "Good."

What a sight it must have been just then to see two maniacs standing on the edge of a building, making out as if death wasn't waiting for them a few stories below. Well, it was waiting for one of us, anyways.

I feared that now would be the opportune time for her crazed buddies to pop out again with their scary knives. "Don't worry. We're not going to do that again. But I am going to give you some inspiration to take my offer."

How?

"You said you want to make sure you have your lighter on you when you die, right? So a certain someone could know that?" Yes. I don't want to write her name again today but I think we all know who that someone is.

I don't know how she did it, but Tallulah was now holding my lighter, smiling wickedly. I demanded to know how she got it away from me. I wanted it back immediately. "Promise to kill us and I'll think about it." No.

Tallulah shook her head, disapprovingly and dropped the lighter down the front of her shirt. I hadn't even noticed her cleavage was visible. Somewhere in there was my Zippo. I felt like a pervert for staring but I wanted what was mine. "Okay, how about just me? Promise to kill just me and I'll give you back your lighter." No! "Wrong answer."

I was not expecting what happened next at all. Tallulah put her arms out and just casually fell backwards. She even managed to give me a small wave goodbye as she fell off the roof. I watched her body hit the pavement below with a sick thud and cracking sound. The back of her head must have busted open because blood spurted out of it on contact and continued to seep out into the parking lot. Her arms and legs were all twisted like a rag doll. She wasn't moving. How could she? She was dead. She had to be.

A mere second or two was all I had to pull myself over the railing and back onto the rooftop before I fainted and ended up joining her down below. Also, I knew I was going to puke and I thought it'd be way out of line to throw up on her corpse from so high up. Not that throwing up on her from any distance was acceptable. I just thought it would be extra fucked up to do it from the factory ledge.

I don't know about the guilt thing but if her goal was to stress me out then she was doing a marvelous job of it. Why couldn't I just kill myself in peace?

After getting all of my puking out of the way I went downstairs to inspect the body. She was still lying in the same spot, surrounded by blood. It was way worse than the stabbings behind the Cracker Barrel. Most dead bodies that were victims of violence are cleaned up more or less before I get my hands on them at work. Unfortunately, I do get the gruesome types sometimes but I maintain a strict focus on restoring their look to the satisfaction of their families and that helps to keep the shock value to a minimum as I work on them. This was different. This was like some over-the-top special effects prop you'd see in a Troma movie. Only it was real.

I fought back the urge to vomit again and noticed something by Tallulah's stomach. It was the outline of my lighter through her shirt. Now, I'm not in the habit of ripping off the dead, but it was my lighter. So I mustered up the balls to crouch down by the body and I put my hand down the front of Tallulah's shirt to retrieve the item.

"If you're feeling for a pulse, your aim is a little off, Guy." I froze in place as she grabbed me by the wrist and I immediately started babbling an explanation about how I was just trying to retrieve my lighter. It all came out with such an erratic stutter that I probably sounded like a cell phone with a bad connection.

"Just help me up and I'll forget about it." Okay. "You should probably take your hand off my tit first." Oh, my God! I didn't even realize I was holding it. How embarrassing.

I released her breast from my grasp and got her to her feet. She was covered in blood but didn't seem to have any injuries. How the fuck? "Thanks, big boy." I tried, unsuccessfully, to ask for my lighter back again.

"Don't be so black and white, Guy. It's unattractive." I just want it back. "Promise me death and I'll promise you your precious little lighter." I can't do that. "Why not?" I can't just kill someone. That's murder. "You did it once already." Yeah, but that was self defense and everyone came back to life so it doesn't count.

"Then don't look at it as murder. Look at it as liberating someone from the pain of living. Look at it as saving someone from life. How's that?" It doesn't really help. "Well I'm covered in blood so I'd like to go home and get cleaned up. Plus it's breezy today and it looks like rain. I don't want to catch pneumonia out here." Why not? Maybe that will kill you then I won't have to. "Tried it already. It just feels like a three day hangover. I'm not going through that again. Jesus, why's it so cold?"

Do you have a car here? "No. I had Kovac drop me off. I was supposed to call him to pick me up but..." She pulled the remains of a broken cell phone from her back pocket. "I don't think I'll be reaching out to touch someone with this any time soon."

I have my car here. I'd be willing to give you a ride. "That...is so sweet of you, Guy. I'd love that. Thank you." Don't mention it. "You know, I think we've had enough adventure for one day. What do you say we go to my place and I'll make us a nice dinner?"

Really?

"Sure. I may be psychotic but I make a mean lasagna." Uh...okay. But I'm not really that hungry, which is weird considering I just puked my weight in vomit a few minutes ago. "Then we'll just have to work up an appetite."

Neither of us really spoke much in the car as I drove. She would just occasionally say "take this exit" or "turn right here." I didn't see that Barracuda out front when we got there so I assumed it was probably her friend's car. The one who was supposed to pick her up.

Now that it was day time and I could get a better look around, Tallulah actually lived in a nice neighborhood. I forget what the area is called. From the outside, her house looked old. Slightly run down but with an odd sense of charm to it. She had only been living there for a few years and bought the house outright. It used to belong to an old couple that had an endless supply of children and grandchildren constantly filling it with laughter, love and enough joyful memories to fill ten lifetimes.

You wouldn't think this used to be a hot spot for happiness when you walked in and the overall dreariness of the place pounced on you instantly. "I bought it specifically because of its history. I thought a home that hosted so many warm, loving scenes would rub off on me. Feed me its positive energy. As you can see, I've clearly rubbed off on the house instead."

It was a fairly big house for one person. I wondered how she was able to afford it. Then again, I never even bothered to ask what she does for a living. I pictured her earning money from selling potions and dream catchers. Maybe people paid her to cast hexes on ex-husbands and landlords they hated.

Apparently, she had an uncle on her dad's side that she had never met but who did really well for himself. He had abandoned the family years ago and no one knew what had become of him until Tallulah received a notice that he had died and left her close to two million dollars. I asked her if she knew how he died and I wish I hadn't because she told me exactly how he died.

The coroner's report stated that he died mainly from a drug overdose. Combined with the fact there was enough alcohol in him to annihilate even Norm Peterson's liver, there were a number of other substances found in his system, including cocaine and Sildenafil Citrate (hard-on drugs.) I can't imagine anyone expecting to live after taking in all that but supposedly that was his thing.

Prostitutes were also his thing, as the last person to see him alive was a lady of the night. She testified that he was already drunk when they went to some dive motel where he started popping pills and snorting cocaine. They had sex for an hour and he was still alive when she left. At some point after he succumbed to all the toxins in his body, someone came into his room and decapitated him. Then they positioned his head on his still erect penis so when the motel manager found him it looked like he was giving himself a blowjob.

81

Can you believe that? That might be the worst thing I've ever heard. This happened in New York City by the way, so keep that in mind the next time you guys want to fly up there for your Times Square and "dirty water dog" fix.

Given this revelation as to the source of her funds, I wanted to eat food even less, but Tallulah didn't seem bothered by it. I barely knew her but look at all the crazy shit I've seen since she came into my life. Who knows what the fuck she's come across in her day?

We sat in the living room where I saw her and her friends trying to kill themselves the last time I was there. That felt a bit awkward, but not as awkward as Tallulah staring at me with a smile and not speaking. I finally asked her what she wanted. "I'm just trying to figure out what a man so handsome and kind could possibly be so depressed about." I'm kind because I was raised that way and I appreciate the compliment but I think you'd find better looking guys in a police lineup.

"Modest too. I like that. So I'll be honest with you, Guy. I didn't bring you here to eat lasagna. I am gonna make it, but later. In the meantime, you and I started something that we didn't get to finish." You're not going to have me try to kill you right now, are you?

"No." She smiled that warm smile again. "There is something I want you to do to me though."

Before I could protest (as if I would have) Tallulah was sitting in my lap, facing me. We started kissing, passionately, like the day I met her. You would probably say I should have nothing to do with this woman and should have just run, run, run the hell out of there but I couldn't help it. It isn't just that I find her beautiful, there's something else. I've found other women to be very attractive and was not interested in them for one reason or another that is so minute compared to the baggage Tallulah comes packed with but she feels so right. I'm probably making a huge mistake (to add to my many others) but there's something for sure there that I have to pursue. If anything, just to find out more about this not dying thing and how it's caused. I hate to think it's something that could happen to me. Hopefully, it's not contagious.

Ten minutes might have went by as we kissed. It could have been hours for all I cared. Then Tallulah kissed the side of my face, working her way to my ear and she whispered, "I want you to take me." It was the sexiest thing I've ever come across. Typical me and my reservations.

Not in the coffin, okay? "Of course not. There's a spare bedroom upstairs. It's very normal." Just point it out.

Much to my surprise I picked Tallulah up and carried her to the second floor, like in some movie. I still can't believe I did that. She seemed to get a kick out of it. I haven't been hitting the gym lately so good thing she doesn't weigh much. I'm just glad I didn't accidentally smash her head into the railing or a wall.

We went into the spare bedroom and she was right, it was very normal. Not much going on in there but there was a mattress. I placed her gently on top of it. I then laid beside her and we kissed for awhile. Our hands were all over each other. This was really happening.

Tallulah then climbed on top of me and said with so much fucking seduction it's unreal, "Now you just lie back and let me take care of everything." I didn't actually have tears in my eyes but at that moment I finally understood how someone could cry because they were happy. It made total sense because Heaven had nothing on that bedroom at that moment.

"I hope you're ready for the most amazing sexual experience you've ever had in your entire life."

Ready or not, I wouldn't have stopped her. The bed, which I didn't realize was a Murphy bed, had other plans though. It retracted at that moment sending us into the wall, where we stayed for the next couple of hours. Somehow I fell asleep. When I woke up it was morning and Tallulah was gone. The bed was flat on the floor again and there was a note nearby. It read, "I'll see you soon, killer. I call you killer because you slay me." She had signed her name below a grouping of X's and O's.

I was impressed by The Honeymooners reference since I don't remember mentioning it was one of my favorite shows, but taking into account what she expected from me in the long run, the note seemed more eerie than light-hearted.

I threw on my clothes (I wasn't naked, just in a shirt and boxers) and got out of there. I came straight home to write you this letter. I'm even more confused now as to what to do. There're a million reasons not to see her again but I can't fight how I feel. I'm probably on a crash course into more misery but if that's the case, maybe it is what I need to realize my demise.

THE FUNERAL PORTRAIT

I just don't know what I've gotten myself into. I don't know if I could do what she asks of me. I'm not a killer. There's only one person I want to kill and it's the poor, lost soul I see in the mirror every day.

Please forgive me for my decisions. I only want to put an end to my hurt, one way or the other. I don't want you to inherit my pain.

Lost,

Guy

WOUNDS ON TOP OF WOUNDS

MAY 7TH

To My Dear Family,

It's been two weeks since I agreed to kill Tallulah and I still don't know if I can go through with it. I've seen her several times since then but she hasn't brought it up again. That's good in some ways. Maybe she's changed her mind or maybe she has a plan that isn't in effect yet. I don't know. I almost wish she would bring it up. It's the elephant in the room for me whenever we're together. Only it feels like the elephant is sitting on my chest, restricting my breathing.

She's been nothing but nice to me too. We even made love a couple of times. Aside from you, Bruno, I doubt you folks want to hear the specifics. I will say, though, they were without a doubt the most amazing sexual experiences I've ever had. She may be cursed with immortality but she's blessed with all kinds of special abilities that would make Madonna blush.

I even got to formally meet her friends, although she never refers to them as friends, only as "the guys." The older one is Kovac. That's the one with the really cool Barracuda. He didn't seem as creepy after I got to talking with him. He definitely still scares me. The initial creepiness is gone is all. He is easily the bitterest person alive, though. He'll crack jokes here and there but his sense of humor is so strange, you're never quite sure if you should laugh or not. It's very sarcastic and pessimistic. He isn't a "the glass if half empty" kind of guy. He's more of a "the glass is completely empty and I want to smash it on your fucking head" kind of guy.

I'm guessing he's about forty-five or so because he mentioned how depressed he got when he hit his forties a few years ago. He has a daughter who he hasn't seen or spoken to in years, which is another source of depression for him. Tallulah says he's tried to reach out to her a couple of times but she wants nothing to do with him. His kid is the only thing in the world that he's proud of. Kovac also mentioned that he's a postal worker, which seems oddly appropriate for him.

"When I'm at work, I can't tell you how many times a day I fantasize about going in there with a shotgun and blowing people's faces right the fuck off. Co-workers, customers--they're all the same to me. Fuck'em all. You want some stamps, old Mrs. Atwater? I'd rather fuck an ant hill than give you one more goddamn roll of stamps. Stupid old bitch and her rotten orange peel smell. I'd start with her. And you know what? I'd do it too. I'd burn down the whole fucking building with everyone in it if I knew for a fact that when the police showed up, they'd put every bullet they have through me and I wouldn't be able to come back. I'd be done and this life would finally fuck off."

That was about a ten on the ol' tension meter. Tallulah says Kovac often talks like that but he'd never do it. Even though she doesn't talk to him, it would break his daughter's heart too much to have a mass murdering father. Not that having a father who kills himself feels great either but at least it's not as bad as taking out your life's discord on people who have nothing to do with your unhappiness. Not even old Mrs. Atwater deserves to have her face shot off.

I miss Mr. Friar. Talk of old people always brings him to mind. I have to stop by his peach stand one of these days soon. That old geezer has no idea how many times he has cheered me up.

The younger guy with the long hair is Gus. He seems to be in his mid-20s. He doesn't talk much but he stares a lot. It's really uncomfortable because sometimes you glance over at him and he's just staring at you, smiling. Other times he is staring a hole into you with this intense look of hatred. He's hard to read. I suspect he is jealous of the attention I get from Tallulah.

I wasn't going to but I asked her if she and Gus had ever been involved. She said that he made advances on her when they first met but she never paid them any mind. I believe her because they get along well but there's some obvious uneasiness there when they interact. He reminds me of myself when

I'm around a woman I find attractive and being intimate with me isn't just the furthest thing from their mind, the thought is completely non-existent. I think he knows that so his time around her, I'm betting, is bittersweet. Boy, do I know that feeling.

I find that although Kovac can be a bit intense, he seems too pre-occupied being tired to actually do some of the stuff he talks about. He is burnt out and worn down. If he was able to die he could probably accomplish the feat by boring himself to death. I'm sure he has tried.

Tallulah is always trying to think up new ways to die. She hasn't been vocal about it on a daily basis but I don't think a day goes by that she doesn't put some thought into figuring out how to end her invincibility. I think Kovac is just hoping she'll figure it out and tell him so he won't have to put forth any effort in solving the mystery.

Gus is different. I don't think Gus cares to figure out what the problem is. He comes across as very reckless and without a care in the world. Not being able to die is probably fun for him. A guy like him would never get tired of the kind of reaction they got from me when they came back to life behind the Cracker Barrel. I'm not so sure he is colossally sad like Tallulah, Gus and I. I think he simply doesn't give a fuck. And that makes him a frightening person to be around.

I don't want to die but then I do. What I mean is, if I had a choice to die based on my current status or live a happy life, I'd take the happy life. Who would want to die otherwise? If every day was a rainbow why would you want to snuff it? I don't think Gus has ever seen a rainbow or would care to. In fact, I think if rainbows were solid tangible things, he'd piss on them.

I tell you this whole thing is so crazy. How am I supposed to kill someone? I've never physically hurt anyone until I met the Undying Trio. And I know this is more like liberation but it's still murder, right? In the eyes of society and God it's still murder, is it not? Would you all think of me as this horrible murderer who couldn't end his life without taking someone else with him? You'd be so ashamed of me. I'm so ashamed of myself that I'm even contemplating this. I just don't know what to do anymore to better motivate my suicide. I've come to terms with the disappointment you will feel when I'm gone and that hurts, a lot. It's the shame that I don't want to blanket you with. You can be disappointed in me. You can even be angry with me but please never be ashamed of me. Even in death, I'd never be able to find peace knowing you were ashamed of me.

I'm a lost soul facing damnation. I beg you not to condemn me to Hell while I still walk this Earth. There are some things worse than death.

I love you tremendously,

Guy

MAY 8TH

To My Dear Family,

I was lying in bed with Tallulah late last night smoking some pot. I know you don't approve of stuff like that but I have gotten high plenty of times in college, I just never told you. See? I still managed to maintain my grade point average. And you thought video games were rotting my brain.

Well, don't be too alarmed. It's not something I do regularly. I can't even remember the last time I smoked a joint and don't say "you wouldn't remember because it's a memory loss drug."

Anyway, we were in bed, feeling nice and I asked her why she wanted to put an end to her life but she wouldn't tell me. Not unless I told her my reason first. I didn't feel like discussing my reasons. I never want to think about my reasons when I'm with Tallulah. I'm too busy enjoying her company, which is starting to worry me. How am I supposed to kill someone I like being around so much? You never hear a newscast with something like that in it.

"Earlier today, Dr. Benjamin Thornhill brutally murdered his wife of thirty years following a romantic dinner for two. When questioned by police as to his motive, Dr. Thornhill had this to say":

'That woman has given me non-stop love and devotion for thirty years. She has never looked at another man. She mothered my three children. She cooked, cleaned and did everything I have ever asked of her without so much as a whimper of protest. She made me smile on a daily basis which often led to laughter. Refused to leave my side when the odds were against me and has seen to it that I've not had a single second of unhappiness enter my life since our eyes first met. I had to put her down.'

"Here's Mitch with the weather."

This whole situation is supposed to be for the better. Why do I feel like it's going to get worse real soon? I can't help but think I will feel even more horrible than I already do on a regular basis and will still be incapable of subtracting myself from the world of the living. That's exactly what I don't need.

It makes me think of those movies where someone does something absolutely terrible and instantly decides they can't live with themselves. Like in Titanic when that crew member shot Fabrizio's friend, Tommy, in the midst of all the chaos on deck and was like, this is fucking crazy. I resign from my position, oh yeah and life too: Bamn! Or when Warden Norton in The Shawshank Redemption realizes he's about to be arrested for his criminal behavior. Damn you, Dufresne! You'll never take me alive, Coppers: Bamn! The same for Leo G. Carroll in Spellbound. He's lost his mind and has done things that he'd never contemplate in the past. I'm the proprietor here! This is my place but if I can't fix you, I'll fix myself: Bamn! Shit, even people in zombie movies sometimes kill themselves before they let the living dead rip into their flesh. I'd probably just stand there, gun in hand, like a fucking moron while a couple of zombies tear my arms off for lunch.

So maybe Tallulah is right. This probably is exactly the type of motivation I need. I can kill her and then be like: I can't believe I just killed someone. What have I done? I'm out of here. Bamn! You know it'd be more like: I can't believe I just killed someone! What have I done? I think I'll hold this gun to my head for a couple of hours, with the safety on of course, and cry about it until I'm badly in need of a Slurpee.

Sigh.

I do want to go through with this. Obviously, it isn't because I harbor any serial killer fantasies I'm just dying to try out. When you're someone like me, who feels the way I do all the time and can't push themselves to make a difference, you begin to get desperate for an answer. I won't enjoy it if I end up doing it that's for sure. Not only because I've grown fond of Tallulah but because it's so cold.

People are killed every day and it just makes me sad because when I think of having to kill a person it seems easier to just leave them alone than take their life. I might not have it in me.

Then after you kill someone you have to deal with the body. Oh shit! I completely didn't think about that. What the fuck am I supposed to do with her body afterwards? I can't put it with the recycling and I'm not driving out to the middle of nowhere at three in the morning to dig a shallow grave. Fuck! How did this major detail slip my mind?

No, it wasn't the weed. I know you're thinking that.

I could make it look like an accident but don't people do stuff like that all the time and somehow the forensics squad traces it back to them? If they can figure out how the fuck King Tut died thousands of years ago, I'm pretty sure they'd be able to tell who killed Tallulah. Goddamn it! This could definitely be a deal breaker. She'll just have to understand. What if I went to jail? Can you imagine? I would want the death penalty so then it'd be out of my hands. I wouldn't actually have to kill myself because the state will do it for me.

It would never happen though. Even if I was sentenced to death I'd probably just be on Death Row for years and years until I die of boredom. Or they'd just give me life and every time I get violently beaten and sodomized in the shower I'd be begging for those fucks to put me out of my misery with a good shiv to the heart. The throat actually. At that point, who the fuck has a heart?

How the hell am I supposed to do this?

Terrified,

Guy

MAY 14TH

To My Dear Parents,

I don't usually let my job get to me as far as emotions go but I must admit this week was pretty tough. We had two funerals that I, for all my attempts, could not stop thinking about.

The first was an old couple: Sam and Marion Kentley. Married for fifty-six years. Madly in love to the very end with a bunch of children, grandchildren and great grandchildren madly in love with them. Still affectionate. Still able to make each other laugh. Found peacefully lying in their bed, dead from natural causes.

The funeral home was never so full before. It seemed like everyone the Kentleys had ever met who were still alive had shown up to pay their respects. I imagine anyone who came in contact with them was treated as nice as anyone can be treated. It's always a shame when the world loses people like that. So many of us are miserable assholes who wouldn't even use our garden hoses to put out someone who has caught fire because that would wreak havoc on the water bill. Most people are just great at disguising their lack of having anything really worth a fuck to smile about. I may not be able to hide my lack of sunny days but I would definitely help someone who has caught fire, even if that meant the highest water bill in all of Florida. That's because, unlike the

95

"every day actors", as I call them, I wouldn't be able to live with myself if I didn't help those in need of saving. I wouldn't be able to sleep at night. I can't live with myself or sleep at night anyway, but I don't pretend to be something I'm not. I know how pathetic I am, but I'd never let someone suffer if I could help it.

These Kentleys, after so many years of being nice to everyone, being nice to each other, teaching their children and grandchildren to love one another and approach the world with a welcoming hand, unconsciously decided they've done all they could. Without planning it (how could you if it was natural causes?) they both went to bed and gently drifted away together. When I went to pick up their bodies with Devlin I noticed right away that they were holding hands. I asked the family if they had done that but aside from several short emotional embraces, they hadn't moved them. Can you believe it? How fucking unreal is that? Is it possible they always held hands when they slept? Maybe but that's unlikely. Somehow, they knew. Even in their sleep, their souls were so connected that they knew their time on Earth was over and they would be moving on. So they took hold of each other's hand one last time with the bodies they occupied to love each other for almost sixty-years. I can think of nothing more amazing. What a beautiful, beautiful way to die.

I wanted so much to cry during their service. I don't think anyone would have noticed since not a single person was without tears in their eyes. A lot of them smiled or giggled fondly as loved ones gave their eulogies, filled with enough happy memories to keep the Neverland flights of Peter Pan and the Lost Boys fueled until the end of time.

Bates would've flipped out though if he spotted me crying. Cold fuck. And Devlin, ignoramus that he is, I'm starting to believe is too dense to notice something he should feel emotional about. He's not a bad guy and he's made a lot of progress at work but talk about oblivious. I think Devlin is the type of person that could drive his car right into a herd of cows and be like, "What the hell are all these cows doing on this farm?" He's not really aware of his surroundings.

The other funeral which really saddened me was for a Mr. Sebastian Alexander. He resided in a retirement community a mile or so from Mr. Friar's. Not a single person showed up for his service. It was scheduled like they normally are and paid for completely by his only living relative--a son up in Boston. Alexander's son was very clear about his not attending the wake or burial but we (and he) assumed other people would come to pay their respects. No.

Hours went by and it was just Bates, Devlin and me sitting around in case someone came in. I spent most of that time staring at the old guy lying in his coffin, wondering how he must have felt at the end. I bet it was the opposite of the Kentley's. He probably felt so lonely, so unloved. Maybe like them he unconsciously decided in his sleep it was time to move on, but not because he had accomplished enough in this life and was ready for the next step of existence, but because there was no point in opening his eyes to face another day. So, so sad.

Devlin and I drove him to Morningside Cemetery the next day to be buried. He was immediately placed in the ground without any hesitation since his burial was also a desolate affair. His son didn't bother arranging for a Priest either so I had the gravediggers wait while I said a few words. Only I couldn't think of anything. I ended up just staring down at the coffin for a few moments until finally I whispered, "I know how you feel" and walked away.

There wasn't anything else going on at work that day so I took an extra long lunch break and decided to see if Mr. Friar was around. It was warm outside, but not too hot and a cool breeze was doing laps around town. It was the kind of day you get maybe ten times the whole year so I figured he might take advantage of the weather and sit by the road with his peaches. I was right.

He had just finished selling a few peaches to a couple of attractive women with really short shorts. I could see in his face he probably wished he could be twenty-five again, at least for one night. There was a lot of life left in the old timer yet. I exchanged smiles with the ladies as they walked by me to their car. Mr. Friar was now enjoying the back view. I think I saw his nostrils flaring.

Once they drove off, I remarked on how good looking his customers were, present company excluded. He said something to the effect of, "If those shorts were any shorter I would've been checking out their peaches instead." I had no idea Friar was capable of such a perverted statement. It still makes me laugh thinking about how unexpected that was.

He told me that he had been thinking about me lately and how down I've been. I always just assumed he never gave me another thought once I was out of view. I asked Mr. Friar (I never called him Eric, and he knows I won't so he stopped insisting I do a long time ago) what was on his mind, concerning me.

THE FUNERAL PORTRAIT

"Today is a beautiful day, Guy. Even a crazy man couldn't argue with that. But as we sit here and marvel at the beauty of a day like this, somewhere, at this very moment, someone is having the worst day of their life." I found that to be kind of depressing.

"Life itself is depressing, Guy. Every one of us has the same ending. There's no escaping it." He hasn't met the company I've been keeping recently.

"But I think if we, as people, can have moments like this every once in a while where everything is beautiful and perfect, it makes life worth living." There was that usual optimism I expected of Mr. Friar. "Well, you know I've had my share of hard knocks. I lost my wife and one of my kids already. I've got one foot in the grave myself. I guess I should be having a hard time but I'm not."

"Why is that?" I asked. I would be really depressed--more depressed--if I lost all my loved ones and had nobody. He still had one son left but, due to his business, he couldn't visit that often. Even the peaches Friar sold were dropped off by one of his son's employees and not personally. If that were me, I'd probably want to...kill myself or something.

"I look at it this way, Guy--from the moment you're born, life is against you. It's just a matter of time before you die. Whether it be long or short, it will happen. Now in my case, I was married to the most wonderful woman ever for forty-two years. She loved me like you wouldn't believe. We had two great kids who couldn't have made me more proud to be their father. Then I lost her and my younger son to cancer earlier than they deserved but for the

99

time I had them, I was the luckiest and happiest man alive. And I know there are tons of people who never even get to feel that kind of joy." I wondered if he missed them though--or if he missed being loved back by them?

"Sure, I miss their company. I miss being able to talk with them, laugh with them--things like that. But as far as being loved, I always feel loved by them. I know wherever they are, they love me. Love's not a physical thing so the love they gave me while they were alive is always in me. I still feel it today." My problems never felt so stupid and trivial before now.

Mr. Friar thought he offended me since I'm usually complaining about something that's got me down and here's a man with very legitimate reasons to be depressed and he's not. He's actually wasting time he could be using in a million different and better ways, to try and cheer me up. I wasn't offended by his words though. I know what he's trying to tell me and it's good. I need to get over certain things and just haven't been strong enough to do so.

"Well, you'll come around. Just remember, if you spend too much time with your head down you're gonna miss out on the good stuff that's right in front of you. Then when you finally look up, it just might be gone. Only hold on to the stuff that makes you smile, everything else treat like a bad dream-- as long as your eyes are open it can never hurt you." I guess I better get my shit together. And it was a good time to do just that because my extra long lunch was about to get me in trouble with Mr. Bates.

I thanked Mr. Friar for the talk (and the free peach he gave me.) Even when he kind of scolded me about my negativity, he still made me feel better.

I hope his remaining son realizes what a good man his father is. Before I left he even told me, "Good luck getting your shit together, Guy."

Even if only on an external level, it really was a beautiful day. I tried to let as much of that as I could seep into my world on the drive back to work. I sure wish you guys were here.

All my love,

Guy

MAY 15TH

To My Dear Family,

So much for getting my shit together. I was late to work and combined with my extra long lunch break the other day, Bates was all over me the second I came through the door. I know I should be flattered that he relies on me so much but it's really annoying sometimes. I often make it sound like it's just him, Devlin and me at work but that's not the case. There's Mrs. Peiser, who handles all the paperwork and phone calls and we have two attendants, Richard and Tim, who aside from preparing the bodies for viewing, do just about everything else. They don't embalm, but if necessary, they can both, clean and dress a body, apply makeup (I rather they didn't because everyone always ends up looking like Divine in Pink Flamingos) and place it in a casket. We even have a hydraulic lift so that it only takes one person to do this, although I prefer it to be a two-man job because things don't always run smoothly.

One of the very worst things you could do is accidentally drop a body on the floor because someone was careless operating the machine. That's right up there, but probably not as bad, as over-embalming. If you put too much fluid it can cause severe swelling of the neck and face, which you won't be able to hide in an open casket viewing. I've never done this myself but I've seen it happen and it makes things a lot harder on the family when they show up and their loved one looks like they're retaining a bathtub's worth of water.

I always fill them out on my own but Bates has been having Richard or Tim assist Devlin with the embalming reports. This includes stuff like taking a log of all the jewelry and personal items with the body. We also have to make note of any discolorations, bruises, cuts, stuff like that. What kind of chemicals and procedures we use also has to be documented. This report is extremely important because it helps protect the funeral home in the event a lawsuit is brought against us by the family of the deceased for whatever reason. Bates is a stickler for this paperwork, you can imagine.

I guess Devlin just doesn't have the eagle eyes yet that the rest of us have for spotting every little detail on a body. I don't think I've ever really shared with you what I do for a living. I mean, you know, more or less, but I never really talk about it. I hope you don't mind if I do. I feel like a total loser all the time so it'd make me feel better if you knew I was at least good at one thing in my stupid life. So here's the lowdown.

After removing every stitch of clothing, bandages, catheters, IV needles and such, we clean the skin, eyes, mouth and other orifices with a strong disinfectant spray. If rigor mortis has set in (death's Viagra) then it can be relieved by manually moving the limbs and head around and massaging the muscles. I hate to think this will be the only massage some people ever get. No, Bruno, no one gets a "happy ending." I know you were thinking it and that's just so insensitive.

Once they're loosened up, I typically shave the face of the deceased. It's obviously more essential if it's the body of a man because they can still suffer from razor burn if I do this after the actual embalming. Regardless, everyone's face gets shaved, whether it be a man, woman or child. Most everyone has some sort of peach fuzz on their face and if we don't get rid of it the makeup tends to collect on this hair and become more noticeable.

Now everything is clean and as fresh as a dead person can be so we begin the process of placing the facial features and the body in the way they will appear in the casket for viewing. There's no way I'd be able to do this after the arterial embalming because everything will be set firmly in place once the formaldehyde reaches all the tissue.

We use a positioning device to make sure that the arms are held in a set position, which typically means hands folded across the stomach. The head is propped up on a head block and I always tilt the head about 15 degrees to the right so that mourners don't have to lean over the coffin to get a good look at the face. No detail is too small. People should be able to focus on grieving and it's important not to let your carelessness distract them from that. Little things go a long way.

One thing Devlin hasn't quiet mastered yet is keeping the eyes closed. I personally think he's a bit weirded out by it. That makes no sense to me considering the other tasks involved in preparing a body for viewing. Now, the traditional way to keep the eyes closed was by placing a bit of cotton between the eye and eyelid. We use small plastic eyecaps though. Often, after death, the eyes tend to sink back into their sockets, so an eyecap is placed on each eyeball. These are like big contact lenses with a textured surface that holds the eyelid in place. And a small amount of stay creme is placed on the eyecap so that the eyelid doesn't dehydrate. If I'm really bored though and have a lot of time to spare I will just sew the eyes shut...

I'm kidding! No one does that, Bruno. I single you out because, even though I'm the one who does this for a living, you insist that is how this task is carried out. I keep telling you, it's just a cool Alice In Chains song, not procedure. However, I have glued stubborn eyes shut before.

There are two ways we secure the mouth of the deceased shut. Either the jaw is tied together using a piece of suture string (just stitches, pretty much) or with a special injector gun. Bates prefers using the suture string. He takes a curved needle with a piece of the string and threads it through the jaw, right below the gums and through the upper jaw into the right nostril. It's then threaded through the septum of the nose into the left nostril and passed back down into the mouth. Then you carefully tie the two ends of the suture string together. If you want a natural appearance you can't tie them too tight. You're already dead, no sense in looking so uptight about it.

Devlin and I always use the injector gun. This gun drives needles with a piece of wire attached to them into the upper and lower jaw and then twists them together. Fast and efficient. We all use mouth formers though, regardless of how we secure the mouth shut. These are like the eyecaps with a textured side that grips onto the lips, but they're shaped like the mouth. A little bit of stay creme is also used on these to prevent dehydration and further holds the lips in place. Not always, but occasionally we'll squeeze a little mastic compound in there to give the mouth a more pleasing, natural shape. That's a paste like caulk. Works wonders. Devlin pretty much skipped over this whole process that time with old Mr. Rittenhouse. That's why the old man's family is scarred for life but received a huge discount in order to calm things down.

Now comes the part that always makes me think of those Phantasm movies--the arterial injection of the embalming fluids. By using the body's own vascular system--arteries, veins, capillaries--embalming fluid flows to all parts of the body, preserving the skin, organs and muscles. The process begins by selecting an artery to inject the fluid and a vein for draining the blood. Sometimes multiple injection/drainage points are needed but the best place is usually on the right side of the body, near the collarbone. That's because the right common carotid artery and the right internal jugular vein are both located here next to each other. Easy access.

You have to make a small incision that's just deep enough to cut the skin. The neater and more precise you are the less chance of creating an unnecessary mess. Also you won't feel like you're desecrating the body by clumsily hacking it up. After that, an aneurysm hook is used to separate the tissue above the artery and vein. The artery is raised above the surface of the skin and two pieces of suture string are passed beneath it to create a ligature to tie off the vessel once the arterial tube is inserted. You do the same thing with the vein.

Each vessel receives a tube for the purpose of injecting or draining fluids. Very carefully, so you don't cut it in half, an incision is made in the artery and an arterial cannula (tube), is inserted towards the heart. The ligature is then tightened to make a seal between the tube and artery. All of this is repeated for the jugular drain tube, only a clear hose is attached to the drain tube and the hose from the embalming machine is connected to the arterial tube.

You can also perform drainage by keeping the vein open using angle forceps. I've been trying to convince Devlin that this is the better way to do it because it allows for clots and blockages to be flushed from the vascular system a lot easier. He just doesn't get it.

On to the chemicals and the reason I always smell like a stale hospital waiting room. We have quite a few different embalming fluids. Pre-injection chemicals help break up those clots I mentioned and condition the vessels. Coinjection chemicals restore dehydrated tissue, correct hard water and fights edema, which is too much fluid in the tissues. Cauterants are very handy because they dry, seal and preserve open wounds.

The most important chemical, of course, is the arterial fluid, which consists of preservatives, germicides, anticoagulants, dyes and perfume. The main ingredient is formaldehyde. I know you've all heard of that before. It's extremely toxic and is a known carcinogen, but it's what works the best. We're very careful with it though. Even the Occupational Safety and Health Administration, regulates its use in funeral homes. Things like exhaust fans in the prep-room and signs warning about the presence of formaldehyde are required. There's a whole bunch of rules and regulations so don't worry, Mom, we're safe.

Some are worse than others. See, the formaldehyde content in arterial fluids is measured by index. That's just the total percentage of actual formaldehyde gas in the fluid. Fluids with an index of 5 to 15 are weaker in terms of firming. 16 to 24 produce a medium firming and 25 or above really stiffens that tissue.

The body gets about one gallon of fluid for every fifty pounds of body weight. Typically, a gallon of fluid is made up of one bottle of arterial fluid, one bottle of coinjection fluid and one bottle of water corrective. Water is used to complete the gallon. Quantities and combinations can change though depending on the condition of the body.

Once I've got the reservoir of one of our Porti-Boys loaded with my concoction we can begin the injection. These embalming machines have two knobs which regulate pressure and the rate of flow. Whoever is embalming can adjust these to ensure the greatest rate of injection into the body. You kind of just do what you think is best here. There's no rule set in stone.

Our machines also have a pulse feature that pumps the fluid by simulating a heartbeat. This alternating pressure is great for avoiding the swelling of tissues. You just flick the switch and the fluids make their way through the hose, arterial tube and into the body. And once the fluid starts to flow into the arterial system, pressure will build up in the entire vascular system, helping the fluid reach all areas of the body and really penetrate the tissues. You'll know that's happening when you see bulging veins throughout the body. The jugular drain tube is normally closed but I open it periodically to allow blood to escape and keep too much pressure from building in the vascular system. If you don't, it could cause swelling. This is really going to gross you out in particular, Bruno, but that drained blood goes directly into the sewer system. I guess I can understand why that would gross you out but hey, isn't the sewer where we dump all of our nasty shit anyway. At least we're not dumping toxic chemicals in there and creating some sort of huge, mutant monster.

There's several ways to tell whether or not a body has gotten enough juice. There are dyes in the arterial fluids that let me know where they've reached or didn't get to. Plus, they help give the body a more life-like appeal. The less you have to rely on the makeup to get a natural appearance the better, I say. If arterial fluid is starting to make its way into the jugular drain tube then you've probably already infiltrated the entire vascular system. And basically if you can feel the firmness taking hold then the fluid has successfully reached the tissues. That's a no-brainer but that doesn't make it any less vital, information wise.

Once you're done with all that, the arterial and jugular tubes are removed. Then you have to tie the vessels closed and use the suture string to seal that incision you made to access the vessels in the first place. You should use some Seal-O-Tite on the incision as well, to prevent any leakage.

I always get excited...well, I wouldn't say excited, but I'm always relieved when I don't have to perform this next step which is dealing with the body cavity. You see, the arterial fluids are for treating the skin, muscles and organs themselves. What's inside those organs though—like urine, bile and whatever—begins to decompose despite the fluids I've already pumped into the rest of the body. Gases and bacteria can build up and cause distention, horrible stenches and purge.

Can you imagine if on top of his mouth becoming slightly ajar, old Mr. Rittenhouse had started drooling, disgusting brown shit out of his mouth? I'd probably be prepping Devlin's body right now because Bates would have definitely killed him. And after all your hard work, you don't want that

109

bacteria spreading to other parts of the body and causing decomposition problems. Not only will you have an angry family to deal with but in all likelihood, a lawsuit as well.

Cavity treatment begins with the aspirating of fluids out of the internal organs in the abdomen and thoracic cavity. We make this happen with the use of a trocar, which is a long metal tube with sharp blades at one end and a connector for a hose at the other. In order to create the suction necessary to accomplish this, you connect the free end of the hose to an electric aspirator. There are also water-powered aspirators, called hydro-aspirators, but we only have the electric kind. The sharp blades of the trocar are then used to pierce through the abdomen, near the belly button. From this entry point I can direct the trocar towards each internal organ, easily piercing them. It's important that you allow the trocar to remain in each organ long enough to suction all the fluids.

Disconnect the hose from the aspirator next and connect it to an adapter that screws directly onto a bottle of cavity fluid. Again, you will have to pierce each organ so that the cavity fluid can flow right into them. It typically takes two bottles of full strength fluid to treat the entire thoracic and abdominal cavities. These cavity fluids are pretty similar to the arterial fluids and contain about the same percentage of formaldehyde. Cavity fluids are slightly more acidic though so they produce faster results and firmer tissues. Our cavity fluids have a fresh, wintergreen scent to them. I guess it's like toothpaste but for the hole in you instead of the hole in your tooth. Once you're done treating the cavities, the trocar is removed and a trocar button is screwed into the hole in the abdomen that you used to access the organs. A trocar button pretty much just looks like a large plastic screw.

Of course, none of this cavity stuff is necessary if the body has been autopsied. That's because the medical examiner removes all the internal organs during an autopsy. Sometimes they place them back in the body or just incinerate them. If they're in there when the body gets to me I remove the viscera (organs and stuff) and place it in a plastic "viscera bag." I let it soak in cavity chemicals while the body cavity is aspirated and then coated with an embalming gel and/or embalming powder. It depends. The treated organs are then either placed back into the body or at the foot end of the casket in a plastic bag. I always rather put the organs back in the body because I'm paranoid a frantic mourner may try to fully open the casket one of these days to take hold of their deceased loved one and unexpectedly discover insides on the outside. Drama.

If we don't return the viscera then we fill the empty cavity with absorbent pads. Either way, the autopsy opening has to be suture closed and sealed. Thus concludes the embalming process. The more you put into it the longer it will keep. I mean, a body is bound to start leaking eventually. You just have to make sure that doesn't happen until well after the viewing. On to the makeup!

If I need a break after the embalming and they're not busy I'll let Tim and Richard, wash the body for me. All the hair has to be washed too to remove any blood or chemicals left over. The body is then thoroughly dried and is ready for its beautification. This is where restorations are done, like rebuilding features, masking sores, abrasions and so forth. We only apply makeup to the face, neck and hands. No sense in putting it anywhere that isn't visible. Normally we use a translucent makeup but if the skin is discolored we'll go with an opaque makeup. I feel like every part of my job is the most important but this is the one aspect I handle with the most sensitivity.

It sounds silly but its hard work sometimes making the makeup look very subtle. If they're male, I try to make the bodies I work on look like they're not wearing any makeup at all. For females, I like to get feedback from the families as to how the deceased styled their makeup. I'll study a picture of them and vigorously strive to recreate their normal look. I always hated when someone passed away who barely even wore so much as lipstick and then you go to their viewing and their face is covered in all this clown whore makeup. Ridiculous. Bates is pretty good at makeup and Devlin is surprisingly proficient as well. Thank goodness for that. I hope to never see another one of those dead drag queens that Tim and Richard seem to have a flair for pumping out.

Fingernails get trimmed here at this point and the hair (if there is any present) gets styled. We do this ourselves most of the time but believe it or not, some people occasionally hire a professional hairdresser to come in and style the hair of their deceased loved one. If I was a barber and got asked to cut some dead guy's hair I would demand a copy of their will first to ensure my name is listed in the "people who get a huge chunk of my money" section. The outfits are chosen by the family (Whether they are provided or they pick out something from our collection.) In addition to these clothes, the ensemble almost always includes underwear, shoes and socks (or occasionally stockings if a dress is being worn.) If there are any difficulties, due to the autopsy or whatever, we place plastic undergarments on the body to prevent leakage.

THE FUNERAL PORTRAIT

Kind of like the big diaper you are always suggesting I wear, Bruno--being the big cry baby that I am.

Finally, we get the body into the casket and pose it in the proper position. At this time, the immediate family will view the body and make any suggestions for changes they feel need to be made. Here, you have to remember not to be offended if they don't initially love your work. Some people cry when they get that first look--the realization setting in. Some people clam up. Some people become totally outspoken, rude assholes because they know you won't lay a smack across their face and tell them to go fuck themselves the next time one of their relatives die and they want you to work your magic. The best thing to do is to remain calm, listen to their thoughts and do your best to make the necessary changes based on what they've told you.

Either Devlin or I need to be present for all viewing services so we can periodically check the body for any unexpected signs of decomposition and immediately take any corrective actions. I look at it this way, it's not perfect but it should be as close to it as possible. You can't preserve someone forever but for that little time the family and friends have with the deceased they should look as much like their normal selves as possible. After all, that image of them lying in that casket will stay with their loved ones forever. You don't want them thinking about how much Aunt Nell looked like Marcel Marceau at the wake. You want them thinking about how peaceful and lovely she looked. Nice thoughts like that can really help out the healing process.

It's a tough job that requires a lot of attention to detail, but I like it enough. I think the fact I have to concentrate so much is a plus. It's the only time my mind is way too busy to think of the usual bullshit that's bringing me down. I'd say the worst thing about it, are the hours. Death doesn't always come at a convenient time so I'm always on call to go pick up a body once the family has arranged its release. It could be the middle of the night or a holiday and I have to drive out to wherever to pick up the deceased and bring them back to the funeral home. Almost always, I have to begin the embalming procedure right away if it's required and as you can see, it's a lengthy process. I don't sleep much anyway but it's so much more tiring being up all night working than it is just lying in bed sulking.

We worked out a system where sometimes I go get the body and sometimes Devlin goes. Occasionally, we send just the attendants, but Bates prefers if one us is there too. It's one of those personal touches Bates likes to provide where the family sees one of the actual Funeral Directors being there during the whole process of retrieving their loved one's body all the way through to the burial (or cremation.) For some reason, even though he's more qualified (on paper), Bates seems to trust Richard and Tim with body retrievals more than Devlin. I think it's a customer service thing. Richard and Tim are way better at dealing with people than Devlin. He's come across as a jerk during some nighttime pickups. When someone just lost a loved one, the last thing you want is some fucking chowder head treating you like you ruined his night with the burden of retrieving your dead uncle.

That's why Bates was pestering me when I got to work. It was my turn and he had to send Richard and Tim by themselves to get Mr. Harry Rogers and Kenneth Walker. Harry was from the same community Mr. Friar lived in. I had met Harry a couple of times while visiting Friar's peach stand. Seemed like a nice enough old man. I imagine Mr. Friar will attend the funeral.

Bates never seemed to believe any of my excuses for either coming in late or taking off work. This particular morning I was late getting up because one of your cats buried my cell phone in their litter box, Bruno. I couldn't hear the alarm going off and had to call my cell from the house phone for five minutes before I was able to locate it. If Bates lived with us, Bruno, I think that scenario would be believable enough. "You have to be more responsible, Guy. We're very busy today. We received a customer first thing this morning and the guys just had to pick up another one. So that makes two you have to prepare since Devlin is unavailable today."

The other pickup, Kenneth Walker, was a young man who died in a car crash. A combination of too much speed and bad road conditions proved to be fatal for the poor fellow. It always disturbs me to work on someone who is younger than me. I guess that feeling will go away as I get older. I hope so.

One of the few things I have in common with Bates is my reactions are very subtle when I'm at work. You always want to seem calm, collective and in total control. Not robotic, just professional. The Kentley and Alexander funerals were very isolated incidents for me. I couldn't help but feel a little bad though when Bates told me about Mr. Rogers. Like I said, I only met him a couple of times but I knew that meant one less friend for Mr. Friar to destroy at checkers. It seemed like every week we had someone in here from either his retirement community or the other two nearby.

"Yeah, if those old bastards keep dropping dead at this pace we may have to start offering group discounts. Now get in the back, Guy, and pump some juice into these door nails." I guess I have even less in common with Bates than I thought.

Mr. Rogers was already cleaned up and prepped. Bates occasionally did this to "stay sharp" as he would say, but he rarely embalmed anymore and never, ever cremated anyone. Even he couldn't explain why he chose not to participate in cremations. Something about it just didn't sit well with him.

So I decided to work on Kenneth Walker first before embalming Mr. Rogers, that way I could take care of them back-to-back. This one was going to take longer than usual because Kenneth had sustained a lot of damage to his face and head. His family was hoping for an open casket service. Luckily Bates told them we'll do our best to restore his appearance but it may not be possible. After prepping him though, I was pretty confident I'd be able to make him presentable enough for an open casket. Once I set his features and filled him with the proper fluids, the makeup and styling would make the cuts and bruises barely noticeable.

I still had the actual embalming to do first though, plus Mr. Rogers afterwards, so I got to it. We're trying out this different chemical now called glutaraldehyde as opposed to regular formaldehyde. It's way less toxic and I think Bates got a good deal on it but so far I find it difficult to gauge its effectiveness. It doesn't seem to create the same amount of firmness, so lately I've been using more than I would of the normal stuff. That could end up being annoying because this was the third time already that I had to refill the machine for a body that needed more juice. Just a little more fluid would do it and the rest I would use for the second body.

THE FUNERAL PORTRAIT

About five seconds after I turned on the machine for another go-round, the phone rang. Mrs. Peiser said I had a call on line one and wouldn't you know it, it was Tallulah. Her first words were, "Hello, Handsome." I tried not to sound too excited and dryly responded. Oh, hello, Miss Leigh. "Surprised to hear from me at work?" Yeah, actually I am. How did you get this number? Did you look it up online? "It's on your sign you big, silly man."

My sign? Are you outside? "Ding! Ding! Ding! And the man wins a prize." What did I win? "You win an all expense paid walk outside your place of work. After arriving at your destination, you will have the luxury of ushering me inside so I can see what you do when you're not trying to jump off of factory rooftops." Okay, but meet me around back instead. I'm not really supposed to have any non-employees in here during the embalming process.

When I opened the back door, Tallulah was waiting for me, wearing unusually bright attire. Bright for her that is. She had on a dress that was off-white with a reddish tint to it. The pattern, I realized after more careful inspection, was a multitude of little dark red skulls. Who would make such a nice summer dress and decorate it with skulls? Red ones at that. Outside of a Tim Burton film or comic book I wouldn't expect to come across any red skulls. I guess I should always expect the unexpected when it concerns Tallulah.

She looked beautiful. Innocent. Even with the cigarette hanging from her lips. I told her that those things would kill her. "Not fast enough, they won't." She tossed it anyway and gave me a nice, long smooch. I made sure no one was around and then snuck her into the funeral home.

My worst nightmare (at work) was realized the second I came back into the prep-room with her. I left the embalming machine running while I went outside to get Tallulah. Now the excess fluid was spewing out all over the place from where I inserted the arterial tube because I left the drainage tube closed. I almost busted my ass too, slipping around, trying to get to it in a hurry and shut it off. Fuck!

"What was that all about?" I told her how I had forgotten to turn off the machine before meeting her outside. "Damn. That sucks." I played it off like it was no big deal and I'd fix it later but I knew I couldn't. Walker was already swollen like a person who's allergic to bees and has been stung fifty times. I would just have to suck it up and tell the family we couldn't get him back to open casket quality. I can't believe I did that. Not even Devlin has done that yet.

Tallulah seemed pretty excited to be in the embalming room, although I doubted it was her first time in one. Just a hunch. She started asking me a bunch of questions about the job and procedures--pretty much everything I already told you. Then she hopped up on the only table not occupied. For some reason, Bates has three embalming tables. I personally think one has served us fine but he insists on the three. I think it's because he feels with several retirement communities nearby we could get slammed with sudden business. I'd rather that not happen but it'd be interesting to see him performing an embalming since I imagine Devlin and I would be busy at the other two tables. He can do it, I know that, but it's been a long time. Somewhere along the line he'd mess up and freak out. That'd be fun to watch. Seems immature of me, I guess, but there aren't many opportunities to get a laugh in at a funeral home.

Tallulah positioned herself on the table as if she were one of the cadavers awaiting my services. "I wish you could embalm me. What a turn on." I could if you wanted me to. Well, I mean, you'd have to be dead first though.

"No. When I finally die I want to be destroyed. I don't want to be planted in the ground. I know it sounds silly but I always thought when you bury someone like me you're poisoning the Earth. As if my lifeless body would harvest sorrow and misery into the dirt until it reaches the surface and infects every living thing."

That's depressing.

"I know. That's why I don't want any traces of me left behind to cause any troubles for good people; happy people. I just want to be forgotten." Well...I wouldn't forget you. How could anyone? "That's very sweet, but hopefully after I'm gone you won't be too far behind." Yeah. Hopefully.

Then she wanted me to show her how I would go about embalming her. Of course, since she was still alive I couldn't carry out the usual routine so I simulated it and then brought over the machine that still had about half of the fluid left in it. I noticed her breathing was becoming heavy and her eyes slowly closed a couple of times.

After all those things happen, I told her, "I'd have to stick the arterial tube in you and fill you full of juice." I held up the tube for her to see and I could swear she moaned, ever so slightly. "Ooh, that looks scary. What's the big, scary man going to do with that? Is the big, scary man going to put that in me?"

Do you want me to put it in you? "Put it in me, baby. I want to feel it deep in me." Like I already explained, the inserting of the arterial tube is a process but I was caught up in the moment so I simply made a small incision up around Tallulah's collarbone, where the neckline of her dress ended. She sucked in air suddenly, making that hissing sound one makes when you rub a wound with alcohol and it stings. I hesitated a little but she begged me not to stop.

I pressed the tube against the opening I had made and slowly pushed it into her. She grunted a bit. Blood poured out onto her dress and the table. Tears dripped down the side of her face but she wasn't crying. That was probably more of an involuntary reaction to the pain. Yet, I couldn't tell if it was pain she was feeling or ecstasy.

Normally, this would go very smoothly. No wondering if I was hurting the person (since they're dead) and no mess. I have to admit, I was quite disappointed in myself at how sloppy my performance was. I asked her how she liked it. "Deeper." I pushed the tube further in and I'm too embarrassed to confirm this but I swear she orgasmed when I did that. "Just like that."

Do you want my fluids in you? "Mmm. Fill me with your fluids, baby?" What a strange and fucked up relationship you must be thinking this is. I agree, it is very strange but it all makes sense to me for some reason. Who am I to deny this beautiful woman the pleasure of my fluids, even if those fluids are for preserving the dead?

I turned on the machine and Tallulah let out a weak giggle. "That tickles." I watched her convulse for a little while (again I couldn't tell if this was pleasure or pain) and she even foamed at the mouth a bit. Within seconds, she was motionless. Dead. I put my ear to her chest and couldn't make out a heartbeat.

Five minutes went by, maybe. All I could do was stare at her for any signs of life. Nothing. I had killed her. I really had killed her. What the fuck was I thinking? Yes, this is where dead people end up--on my embalming table, but they're usually dead before I put them there. This was so bad. How was I going to explain this to Bates or anyone that might walk in for that matter? What was I going to do with her body? Or her car which was parked around back? Someone was going to notice it eventually.

I began to panic and pulled the tube of out of Tallulah, placing it on the table beside her. I noticed some drops of blood on the floor that must have spurted out from that incision I made. How was this even possible? I was never this careless with a body. And now that the body in question was alive before I got my hands on it, there was evidence just lying about.

I grabbed a bottle of disinfectant and sprayed the floor, wiping up the blood. Just as it was clean, a giant splash of vomit hit the floor, getting most of my back and head on its way down. It felt really gross to move even an inch but I turned my head to see Tallulah, leaning over the table, after discharging the most puke I've ever seen come out of someone in one shot. She laid on her side, head propped up from leaning on her elbow, like a sexy centerfold, only she had vomit and glutaraldehyde dripping from her chin.

121

"I've made up my mind. I definitely don't want to be embalmed." I was lucky in the sense that when I fainted then and there, I did so with very minimal noise. Tallulah says I have to be the most squeamish undertaker ever. I'd like to see how even the most seasoned Funeral Director deals with their subject suddenly coming back to life. Unless their last name is Frankenstein, I would guess most of them would piss their pants. Me--I faint. Yes, even though I knew it was a possibility already that she'd rise from the dead, I still fainted. Some things are harder to get used to than others.

In Too Deep Now,

Guy

ODE TO THE WEIGHT ON MY SHOULDERS

MAY 23RD

To My Dear Parents,

Bruno seems to have noticed my changes over the past month. I used to think he was pretty oblivious to my moods but I guess not. I wouldn't go as far as to say I've been tap dancing around the house but I'm visibly happier. Even getting the occasional pie to the face doesn't bother me as much. You should have seen his expression when he hit me with a saucer full of banana cream and I mentioned how the bakery was getting cheap with the cherries. I could tell that seriously pissed him off because he just scowled at my pie covered face and ignored me for the rest of the day. I knew pretending I wasn't even aware of what type of pie it was would burn him up. It was pretty funny.

Even funnier is how I notice him noticing me every day now. I think he's confused and is trying to figure out what's going on without actually asking. I've yet to tell him about Tallulah, that's why.

I probably won't bother telling him about Tallulah either. He'll find out about her sooner or later when you all read these letters but for now, Bruno is the last person I'd consider discussing my love life with. I hate the term "love life." It only makes sense if the people involved are in love. I know it's just a term, not meant to be taken so literally but fuck it. I'm in one of those, not wanting to put up with stupid shit kind of moods right now and I think the term "love life" is fucking bullshit.

Sorry to be so harsh but it's annoying. What if you're dating someone and you've become more emotionally attached to them than they are to you? A person says, "Hey how's your love life?" Well, it's funny that you ask me that because I'm seeing someone right now, who I've fallen in love with but they don't love me. They could in the future perhaps, but they're not there yet. So it's more of a love half-life. I'm hoping for a full blown love life someday but that's really up to the other person now, isn't it? Are you about done fixing my toilet?

I'm just venting. Despite my occasionally faint happiness (that is really cramping Bruno's style) things are not going so great with Tallulah. I'm having a much harder time dealing with this mercy killing thing than she thinks. I've already murdered her and Gus and although they are both still walking around as if that never happened it doesn't take away from how I felt during it. You know how when you're really worried about something, like you left the gas on or you're awaiting test results from the doctor, then you discover the house hasn't exploded and your doctor tells you your one night stand didn't reward you with gonorrhea. You're instantly relieved and all the previous stress is nowhere to be found. Killing someone, even though they come back to life, isn't like that at all. Not for me at least.

I still feel every bit of the anxiety and nausea that consumed me when I initially thought I murdered Tallulah and Gus. It hasn't gone away and I don't think it plans to. And I hate to go on and on and on about how all this feels but go out and kill someone then tell me it didn't completely turn your whole world upside down.

In other news:

There was a really nice day again last week. One of those perfect days that Mr. Friar spoke of. Tallulah and I had decided to go sit in the park with some ice cream cones. I was already annoyed because we had planned to do this the day before, yet she tried to kill herself again with a bowl of assorted medication (again.) Mostly antibiotics. Like everything else, it didn't do the trick, but it took away her sense of taste. When I asked her how her ice cream was she said, "I don't know. I can't really taste it. Come to think of it, I can't really feel it either. Why bother?" With that, she casually tossed the ice cream cone behind her where it was undoubtedly covered in ants right away. I did my best to appear fine the whole time but when we got back into the car she had had enough of my grim mug.

"What's the matter?"

I don't think I can do this.

"What? Kill me?"

Yes.

"You already did it once."

I know and it's really fucking with my head.

"Look, Guy, I don't expect you to completely figure me out and the way I work. In fact, you're probably better off not knowing any more about me than you already do. What I do hope you understand is that I can't go on like this and all I'm asking for is your help in setting me free."

I can't set you free, Tallulah. Don't you understand? It's murder!

"I told you, it's not murder. It's justice. It's helping out a friend so they can be happy. If you loved someone, wouldn't you want to help them out no matter what they asked of you?

I don't love you. (It hurt so fucking much to say that.)

"I know. You love Constance."

I never told you about her.

"Yeah, you did. That first night we spent together you kept mumbling her name in your sleep. You kept begging her to come back to you. You said you would do anything for her if she only came back."

I...

"You cry in your sleep too. Did you know that?"

…

"Hey, at least you can sleep. I don't remember the last time I slept through a whole night without having to take a pharmacy's worth of drugs."

Look, Tallulah, what happened with Constance and me is none of your business.

"You're right. It isn't. But I thought we could help each other and I'm sorry for thinking that. I really am. I'm a girl who's made one wrong decision after another her whole life. What's one more?"

Tallulah, I'm sorry. It's just hard.

"Oh, and this is easy?! You know what, Guy? I don't want your fucking help. I don't want your friendship. I don't want your bullshit. I don't want anything but for you to leave me the fuck alone so I can figure out how to die on my own."

It's not like that.

"Go! Go and run to your precious little Constance so she can remind you of how miserable you are and maybe this time you won't be such a fucking pussy and you'll jump. Have a nice death, asshole."

A second later she was slamming my car door shut and running off. I don't even know where she went but she was gone from sight. It was like she vanished into thin air. I looked in every direction and there was no sign of her. I'm just glad I was at a red light when she got out. Something tells me she would have gotten out at the same point, even if I was still driving at the time. Congratulate me. I just figured out a way to make myself feel even worse than I already normally do. Go me.

When I got home I didn't know what to do with myself. I was surprised that I even went straight home without stopping off at the factory rooftop first. I tried calling Tallulah a couple of times but she didn't answer. I soon found myself sitting on the floor in the bathroom, crying. I feel like even if I lock my bedroom door, Bruno manages to get in so the bathroom is the only place I get any privacy. (Sort of.) I needed it too since Bruno was sitting out in the living room, playing video games, with an iguana sitting on his head and a cat at his feet.

He was drinking beer so it was just a matter time before he wanted in. Beer goes through him like you wouldn't believe. "Hey, you wanna hurry it

127

up in there?! I'm gonna piss all over myself again." Be right out. "If you don't get out of there right now I'm gonna take a big shit on your pillow. I mean it." I'll be right out, I said!

I've seen Bruno when he isn't expecting me to talk back to him. His eyes bulge in surprise but it quickly morphs into rage. That's exactly how I imagine he reacted when I yelled back just then. He must have accidentally kicked the cat as he was storming over to the bathroom because I heard it screech. Then came the pounding on the door.

"Don't take that tone of voice with me, goddamnit! I'll kick this door in and stick this iguana up your ass. Who the fuck do you think you are?" And then he kicked the door, luckily not hard enough to open it. "Fucking depressing jerk! Grow up already!"

Then this poster boy for maturity, brother of mine, retreats back to the couch where he is more than likely further enraged by the fact that he forgot to pause his game prior to putting me in my place. Now he has to start all over because his character has died and the score plus achievements he was aiming for are ruined. Meanwhile, I'm writhing in pain on the floor of the bathroom, while my shaky hand holds that picture of Constance and me. It's stained with my tears.

Is it so wrong to love someone? Why am I being punished for wanting to love someone? I have no meaning. I want to have meaning. I want to be the best thing that ever happened to someone.

THE FUNERAL PORTRAIT

I constantly feel like the worst. Even for you guys. You've probably had headaches that were more enjoyable than the moment of my birth. Too bad at least one of you didn't have a headache the day I was conceived. Oh well, I love you both very much.

Not the best son,

Guy

MAY 30TH

To My Dear Family,

It's been about a week since the prettiest girl in Florida got out of my car and ran away. I've thought about her a lot since then. Even at work now, thanks to the whole embalming incident, I can't get her out of my mind. I didn't even want her near my sacred factory ledge before and now she's infected every aspect of my life. I thought it was hard just having one woman hate me. Two is indescribable.

I did go to the factory a couple of times this past week to see if I'd be able to let go and make a nice bloody red Rorschach test on the pavement where my head used to be. Secretly, I went to the glass factory hoping Tallulah would show up and let me apologize to her. After a few days I would have even welcomed running into Kovac or Gus. Kovac at least. Gus still scares me.

My only visitors on the roof were a couple of sparrows. They ignored me as well. Shit, even the Grim Reaper's got better things to do.

I hit the breaking point finally when I went back to Constance's job. It was a really stupid thing to do. I know. I've based my whole life around doing stupid things, so there. It was raining really hard when I got there. I didn't necessarily plan on confronting her. (With what?) I just had to see her.

The last thing I wanted was for her to call the police on me so I stood behind a tree in the parking lot, where I could see her through the restaurant windows. The rain must've kept people home that day because she wasn't that busy. She made polite chit chat with the occupants at each of her tables. If I didn't know any better I'd say she was enjoying herself. All of her customers got a smile out of her, but some even managed to get a laugh as well. One guy hit the jackpot and got a phone number out of her. At least that's what it looked like. It's usually the customer that signs something and hands it to the waitress, not the other way around.

How I must have looked. Standing behind a tree in a downpour, holding onto the only picture that proves, at one point, Constance and I were a "thing." Crying always felt better in the rain.

After a little while I realized how fucking crazy I would appear if spotted, not just by Constance but by anyone. Besides, I had seen enough. Some people are gluttons for punishment. I'm a downright junkie.

I got in my car, soaking wet, and started driving, not sure exactly where I was going. An hour later I pulled into Tallulah's driveway. Her car was parked outside and thankfully only her car.

It was still storming when I rang the doorbell with a wet finger. No response. This time I knocked on the door. I yelled out, "Tallulah, are you home? It's me, Guy!" No response. I tried the doorknob and it wasn't locked.

Now, I don't think it's cool to just walk into someone's house, uninvited and all but I really needed to see her.

Slowly making my way through the downstairs area I called her name again. Suddenly, she emerged from the kitchen. I froze in place as did she. An eternity of us just staring at each other went by. I had to avert my eyes to speak. I told her...

Look, I just wanted to say I'm sorry. I don't want to hurt you anymore than you've been hurt already. I'm really, very sorry. I've just been so selfish that I couldn't think about how much worse you've had it.

No response.

I know ending it all is the only thing that'll make you happy. I also know that ending it all is probably the only thing that will make me happy too because I can't live like this anymore. But what's really sad is I know I'm not weak enough to have the strength to do what I need to do. So I've decided to help you...and maybe afterwards, I'll have the courage to finally jump.

No response.

So if you'll have me, I would love to help you die.

Subtle smile but no response.

I really wish you would say something.

Tallulah began looking around the room until she spotted some paper and a pen. Without speaking, she wrote out a note and handed it to me. It read: "I can't speak because I just swallowed a bunch of bleach and glued my mouth shut so that I can't throw it up."

Very creative. Tallulah shrugged and smiled as much as the glue allowed her to right before passing out. At least it wasn't super-glue.

Doing What I Think Is Best,

Guy

THE JOYS OF CLINICAL DEPRESSION

JUNE 1ST

To My Dear Family,

I am officially done with Dr. Petersen. I don't mean in a I'm cured or I finished some sort of eight week course way or something--I mean I will never set foot in that man's office again, because I don't need him. He would agree I am beyond his reach.

Yesterday I went to my final session and he asked me how my week had been. Fifty/fifty, I told him. He didn't understand so I explained that I had been in a lot of pain the past few days but now I was more committed to working on making the sadness go away. He was excited about my plan until I told him the first order of business was to immediately stop coming to him.

That dickless turd actually made me repeat myself. I find it hard to believe that he's never had a patient bail on him. He said, "You really think this will make you better?" Definitely.

"I'm sorry, Guy, but I'm going to have to disagree with you." That's all right. I knew he would. You see, I don't need his advice or his pills to feel better. There's nothing wrong with my mind. It's only sadness.

"Yes, you're excessively sad, Guy, and you need help." Only the thought of walking out of his office makes me happy when I'm around him. I don't need a doctor. Sick people need doctors. Crazy people need them. I'm neither. I'm just depressed. It's people like Dr. Petersen who make that such a taboo.

"It's not healthy to be so depressed." Who says? Do you realize that many of the greatest artists and performers throughout history, who have enhanced the lives of countless people, were the most miserable sons of bitches alive? True story.

"Yes. I know artists are sometimes inspired by sadness but that's no excuse to embrace that emotion." Am I sick for looking up to tortured souls? Asshole Petersen said he wouldn't encourage it. You should have seen him squirming in his chair though when I brought up his wife.

His wife--I can't believe someone married this fucking jerk--is a writer. I got a hold of one of her books and noticed the dedication read: Dedicated to Sylvia Plath for channeling your pain into inspiration for us all. My written words would not exist without yours.

Mrs. Petersen has based what she does for a living on one of the most despondent--albeit brilliant--women to ever jot down what was on her mind. A woman who actually committed suicide. Why doesn't the great doctor think his own wife is sick for looking up to such a person?

"What's your point, Guy?" My point is that Petersen spends his whole fucking life telling other people what's wrong with theirs. On top of that, we overpay him to be ridiculed. Does he ever tell his patients that it's not their fault they're so fucked up? Does he ever tell them that perhaps nothing is wrong with them and they're just the victims of other people's rage and evil?

The good doctor was so uneasy that he refused to look at me. I asked him to and when he didn't I asked him again, yelling this time. I told him that sadness is all I know. I'm comfortable wearing it and that brings me peace. That makes me happy in my way. To be able to accept my shitty life is the best medicine I've ever taken. Now when I die, I won't have to feel so goddamn guilty about it.

I know you will be sad when I die and I am sorry for that but I can't feel guilty about it. It's what I want. It's what will make me completely happy and I know my happiness is what matters most to you. Petersen doesn't get that. He only focuses on what will make everyone around his patients happy, he just doesn't realize it. He can't save me.

Right before I left his office, I saw a look on his face that I've never seen. He looked like a man who'd spent years on his knees, praying and serving his religion only to discover there was no God. Very seriously, he told me he was sorry. I couldn't believe the bastard understood what I was saying and let me leave without more of a fight.

In some ways, I felt sorry for him at that moment. A lot of people would look at his diplomas, certificates, treatment history, etc. and proclaim him to be a very successful man but in that one moment, I saw in his face that they would be very wrong.

He is the real failure. Not me.

Embracing Emptiness,

Guy

JUNE 2ND

To My Dear Family,

I told you I was committed to doing whatever I needed to do in order for this sadness to quit harassing me. I need to give myself that push that in turn will push me back and over the rooftop ledge. It's got to work.

I went over to Tallulah's last night with a bottle of champagne and some flowers to celebrate our venture together. She was completely taken aback. "Oh, my God! That is so sweet. Come in." I gave her the flowers and followed her through the living room. "I'll go put these in some water and get glasses. Make yourself comfortable. You know where every--"

She didn't get to finish the sentence because I cut her off by smashing the champagne bottle on her head. It cut her pretty badly and she fell to her knees, but I just ignored all this. I retrieved a clear plastic bag from my pocket and pulled it over Tallulah's head in order to suffocate her. I knew I must've been clenching it really tight because the bag was filling up with blood from her wound and none of it was spilling out.

Tallulah was squirming a lot, gasping for air but I couldn't stop. This is what she wanted. As she choked, Tallulah spouted off a handful of words in between the gagging sounds. "I...think...this...is it." In a few moments she was dead. I let her body fall to the floor hard like a rock-filled pillowcase. I don't know how long I was standing over her, struggling to breathe myself.

This was the first time that I had truly meant to kill her. The embalming thing was almost like a "what would happen if", kind of scenario. Obviously, what I did there would kill her but I wasn't thinking that at the time. This was different. This was premeditated.

I hurried over to the kitchen to down some water with the aspirins I had on me. I gagged a little but was able to keep from puking. I could see her lifeless legs on the floor, sticking out from behind the couch. The silence was threatening to break my composure.

It didn't last long though. I couldn't see her face but when she spoke, you could tell she hadn't taken the bag off of her head yet. "That was so sweet of you to try and kill me right away." While I still had the nerve I grabbed the first thing in the kitchen I could find and hurried back into the living room.

"Is that a rolling--" That's all she was able to get out before I brought that same rolling pin down on her over and over again. It wasn't so bad until the bag broke open and I could see my handy work. Vomiting was beyond preventing at that point. So was passing out.

Of course when I finally woke up, Tallulah looked as if I had only kissed her upon arrival instead of strangling and bludgeoning her to death a couple of times. She came over and gave me a hug and smooch and said, "Dinner will be ready in a few, killer."

Amazing. I wonder what else she is capable of surviving.

Determined,

Guy

JUNE 5TH

To My Dear Family,

This woman really does not die! It's scary and amazing to watch. I filled a bathtub at her place with water and then held her head in it for at least five minutes. She twitched a lot but finally went completely limp after a minute. I could never hold my breath that long on a good day. I knew she was dead, but kept her submerged until she came back to life. I guess she wasn't expecting to wake up with her head still underwater, because she kicked and thrashed around more violently the second time.

After she died again, I positioned her body in the tub so she was sitting with her head above water. As I waited for her to come back I plugged in an old radio I found in the garage. As soon as Tallulah's eyes opened I tossed the radio into the tub with her.

I've seen countless people get killed in movies this way but it was nothing like that for real. It was quick and very frightening, seeing her react to the electricity. It hurt just to watch so I imagine she was in considerable pain as it happened. It also killed the power in the whole house, so I had to find the fuse box and get everything in working order again. I made sure to carefully remove the radio from the tub first.

By the time I got back to the bathroom, Tallulah was already toweling her hair. She confessed that the radio had been a nice and unexpected treat, even though it had hurt like a bitch. The only complaint Tallulah made was that she wished I had told her about the radio in advance. Of course I had wanted it to be a surprise that's why I never mentioned it. Tallulah said electricity is a tricky thing and she has always liked to make special preparations before attempting to commit suicide with its assistance.

Apparently that means to use the potty because she was terrified of pissing herself (or worse) while being fried in the tub. I could understand this concern. I'd be pretty embarrassed if I died and my body decided the last thing it was going to do was rid itself of all those tacos I ate for lunch. Not cool. It's like those people who accidentally hang themselves while jerking off with a rope tied around their neck. Not the best way to spend your final moments or be discovered by loved ones; police; etc. People can be so judgmental.

I brought up the idea of dismemberment, decapitation and burning her alive. She already had tried them all and didn't want to give them a second shot. Dismemberment was weird, she told me, because lost body parts either grew back or reattached themselves if you held them to your body.

Decapitation was even stranger because you didn't grow a new head. Instead, your detached head kept coming back to life but would die again after a couple of seconds when it realized it was not connected to your body. She recounted how once, to amuse himself, Gus annoyingly withheld her and Kovac's heads from their bodies for an hour before he put them close enough to reconnect. That would annoy me too. And I'd be worried about what he did with my head while it was waiting to come back to life.

142

Fire was out as well because she said her body would try to heal itself sometimes while she was still ablaze and it hurt like a kick in the ass from a steel toe elf shoe. (Her words.) So I opted to go behind the glass factory with a bunch of apples, a bow and some arrows. William Tell was to be the game and just guess who had to place the apples on their head.

She didn't really care either way but I made Tallulah wear a blindfold and tied her hands behind her back to add more, for lack of a better term, fanfare to the whole ordeal. She even had me put a lit cigarette in her mouth as a last request. For some reason she spoke in a French accent when she requested this. I'm not sure why but it was cute.

I was completely unaware of my hidden talents, as I pierced three apples in a row without getting her. I'd be a liar if I said I wasn't excited about this. When I thought of this scenario I figured the first arrow I shot would stick Tallulah, no matter how much I aimed for the apple. I guess the steady hands I must possess for work carried over to archery.

After the third one, Tallulah's reaction, standing there blindfolded with the cigarette hanging off of her bottom lip, was "Are you serious? I mean, are you actually aiming for the apples, Guy?" I was.

"Well if you keep up the Robin Hood-like accuracy, darling, we're going to run out of fruit. Now if you're aim is that good, could you be a lamb and go for my throat, please? That would be super."

I took careful aim, not making a sound. She thought I left or was ignoring her. "Guy? Are you still there? Did I hurt your feelings or something? I'm sorry. I'm anxious to face my execution." Wait no longer, I whispered and then released the arrow I had lined up with her neck. It struck with enough force to stick out of the back.

Tallulah made these awful gargling sounds and a tremendous amount of blood spewed from her throat and mouth. After she went down I removed the arrow and the girl was back up in no time at all. She said my archery skills made her panties damp with excitement (Miss Leigh definitely has a way with words) and she insisted I try shooting her again.

The next arrow ended up in her left eye. I admired my precision for half a second when I realized it hadn't killed her. She fell down and was crying (out of her good eye) and squirming in pain. I ran over and pulled the arrow out in one swift motion. The blindfold and what was left of her eye came along with it. Someone had to have heard the scream she unleashed--the whole state, probably.

Luckily she recovered pretty quickly and I untied her. I was scared to look at her and see an empty socket where one of her lovely eyes had been. I was relieved though to see that she had both peepers intact. Truly amazing.

"I don't know about you, Guy, but I'm fucking hor-nay." I never know what will turn this strange, strange woman on but I'm not complaining. After what we did upon returning to her house, what man could?

Greetings from Sherwood Forest,

THE FUNERAL PORTRAIT

Guy

JUNE 7TH

To My Dear Family,

There were some pretty intense conditions here today. Lots of angry winds, steel rain and harsh lightning. Beach weather for sure. That's exactly where I spent my afternoon too, believe it or not. Obviously, not soaking in the sun, but hoping for a casualty.

The massive storm clouds were already hovering in the early morning, stirring themselves into a frenzy, so I made a quick run to a couple of stores. I was able to score a pretty decent Pickelhaube at a pawn shop. A Pickelhaube is one of those German helmets with a metal spike sticking up on top. They always make me picture a biker gang, lead by a humongous gorilla of a man, with a name like Baron Something. And they're all wearing these helmets but his is the most sinister.

So I took the helmet, stripped the inside of its padding then went to collect Tallulah at her place. It was already pouring when we got to the beach. The surrounding lightning was as vicious sounding as I've ever heard it. I made sure to find a safe spot where I'd be out of harm's way but could still see the beach. Then Tallulah strapped the helmet onto her head and went running like a madwoman along the shore, kicking up sand and water as the tide rolled in.

This went on for a couple of minutes until finally a magnificent bolt of lightning struck the spike of Tallulah's helmet. I gasped so suddenly I let loose a tremendous belch. I felt it but I couldn't hear it over the loud crash. I guess I didn't actually expect this idea to work.

Tallulah got thrown back a bit, away from the water, which was good because the last thing I wanted was her body to get swept out to sea. There was no way I was going to go swimming after her in that weather.

All I could do was watch and wait. About four minutes had passed and I was beginning to think she really was dead this time but then I noticed some movement. Tallulah was slow getting up but she got to her feet. Parts of her clothing were burned right off of her. She turned toward me, with a great big smile and started waving. I began laughing uncontrollably and couldn't stop. It just seemed like such a ridiculous gesture after being struck by lightning. And I couldn't decide what was funnier, the absurdity of her casual reaction after coming back to life or the fact she hadn't noticed that enough of her shirt had burned away to expose one of her breasts when she waved.

She wasn't dead but she looked really happy. I think she just really appreciated the effort I was making into thinking up different ways she could die. You'd say we were crazy but somehow, this was fun for us. I watched Tallulah look out over the troubled waters and I knew she had to be smiling.

It was an exhilarating moment, I'm sure. Then she gave me another wave and another much appreciated flashing of her boob. As she trotted back to where I was she did a cartwheel, which lent her such innocence despite the partial nudity. I couldn't stop smiling just observing this wonderful, mysterious creature.

Her second cartwheel was cut short when a second bolt of lightning struck just a few feet away from her. She screamed something to the effect of holy fuckin' crap and hauled ass to where I was. We held each other and laughed for such a long time before she kissed me and said, "I'd love for you to have me right now but I feel like I'm sportin' an electrical outlet down there at the moment, if you know what I mean. Best not to plug anything into it. Let's get some burgers instead." I'm almost starting to wish she never dies. She always seems to come back to life in heat.

Before I could ask, she informed me this was an occurrence that only took place with her and I. "I don't think Kovac's had the energy to maintain an erection for years, plus, ew! And Gus, ha! He wishes." Wouldn't that be my luck? I finally meet a woman that understands me and enjoys every second she's in my company and I'm trying to kill her. Go figure.

I Ate Too Many Cheeseburgers,
Guy

JUNE 9TH

To My Dear Family,

I had a really long day at work today so I'm exhausted. It was damn near impossible to concentrate because I couldn't stop thinking of ways to kill Tallulah. A few interesting ways came to mind but nothing spectacular.

I did meet up with her afterwards though to try at least one option before calling it a night. I don't know how she got it up there without being noticed but Tallulah managed to smuggle a store shopping cart up to the roof of this multi-level parking lot. This lot was predominately used when there were big events in the area so it was virtually empty tonight, seeing as nothing noteworthy was going on.

By the time I had gotten to her she had made a makeshift ramp that lead to the edge of the roof. It wasn't the craftiest thing I've ever seen but it served its purpose. The plan was to put Tallulah in the shopping cart and then push it as fast as I could up the ramp and into the air where she would hopefully land in the loading dock area of the warehouse next door. I didn't think it was possible but Tallulah barely weighs more than the shopping cart she stole.

It was pitch black in that loading dock area so I wouldn't be able to see how she landed. I'd have to wait and listen for her resurrection or lack thereof.

149

The cart would certainly make enough noise. Hopefully, if she did get up, we'd be able to get out of there before the lot's security guard got wise. Of course, that's only if he's able to hear the crash of Tallulah's flight over all that snoring he was doing in his little booth.

Tallulah was now positioned in the cart. I think I should mention that this fascinating woman that I was about to push to her hopeful doom made it a point to wear a vintage leather, aviator's pilot hat and goggles for the occasion. It made her look like one of those old pictures of Amelia Earhart. She even had one of those long, white scarves wrapped around her neck. What a character.

We counted down from ten and then I gave it all I had, which didn't seem like much after the tiring work day. It was enough though because she easily cleared the alley and landed in the dark of the loading dock with a mighty crash. She had started to say, "I'm the King of the--", but didn't leave herself enough air time to finish.

Nothing from the security guard. I had the urge to check his pulse on the way out to make sure he wasn't dead. How did he not hear that entire racket? I stared down into the loading dock for any signs of Tallulah. I thought I made out the cart in the dark but couldn't tell if Tallulah was still in or at least around it.

"I'm alive. I lost one of my shoes."

I helped her find her missing footwear in less than five minutes. We also checked out the cart which held up pretty well, considering the impact it took.

150

THE FUNERAL PORTRAIT

I'll have to remember that the next time I'm speeding down aisle three and some old crone tries to cut off my cart with hers so she can get to that last box of shredded wheat faster--as if that was what I was going for.

Anyway, I'm really drained and I need to get to bed before I'm so tired that I can't fall asleep. I hate when that happens. I just wanted to fill you in on the latest death-defying antics of one Miss Tallulah Leigh.

All my love,

Guy

JUNE 13TH

To My Dear Family,

Tallulah and I decided to take a break from trying to kill her for a few days. That suits me fine because it's a lot of hard work with no results. I figured we would just take it easy and hang out but yesterday I got dragged along to such a crappy situation, my head still hurts thinking about it.

I was at Tallulah's when Gus and Kovac came over. The both of them had been out all day trying to commit suicide with no luck. They brought over some pizza and wanted us to go with them somewhere when we were finished eating. I really didn't want to go, especially since they both kept giggling amongst themselves. You know when you just have a bad feeling about something?

It was already dark when we got into Kovac's car and took off. It was either anxiety or the cheese from that pizza but my stomach was tied in a knot. As cool as I found it to be, the last place I wanted to be at that moment was in Kovac's Barracuda. It was made all the more awkward by the fact Gus clearly noticed the closeness Tallulah and I now had. He would make rude comments like, "You guys are a perfect pair, just like my balls" and "So why is it you haven't killed yourself yet, Guy? If I were you, I would have blown my fucking head off already. I can get you a gun right now if you want." That fucking asshole.

Around nine o'clock we pulled up to an outdoor basketball court. It was well lit and a full court game was going on, with some spectators on the side that looked to be additional players waiting for their turn. There was also a handful of what I assume were girlfriends. Tallulah seemed just as confused as I was. "You guys planning to do some shooting around?" she asked. More giggling.

Kovac turned around to face us with this mischievous grin. "Oh, we're hoping for some shooting, Lulu, but not the kind you're thinking of. Tell'em, Gus." Now Gus had the "up to no good" smile on his face. "What do all of those guys playing basketball, not have in common?" What a stupid question. There could be a million things they didn't have in common. They could've all had different names. None of them seemed to be wearing the same sneakers. For all I knew they could have all disagreed on which movie in the Friday The 13th franchise was the best. (It's Friday The 13th - Part 4: The Final Friday, by the way)

"None of them are white." That would be something they do have in common, Einstein. "And what do people who aren't white hate the most?" Another stupid question with endless possibilities. The first answer that came to my mind was the use of the word "brunch." "That's a good answer but I was thinking more along the lines of a racist." What a fucking moron! It doesn't matter what nationality you are when it comes to racists. You can hate a racist no matter what you are. I'm starting to think maybe Gus is just too stupid to die, the way some people are too stupid to live.

"Well, I know one thing--if you're not white the last thing you want to see is one of these." Gus then pulled off his shirt and showed us a huge swastika he had drawn on his chest with a black permanent marker. He and Kovac were near tears with laughter. I was glad to see Tallulah was just as annoyed and unimpressed as I was. Especially since Gus himself, wasn't white. I think he's Chilean, but I'm not sure.

"I just figured we're always trying to off ourselves alone or amongst each other, I thought I'd bring some other people into the mix like we did with you, Guy, but on a larger scale. It might make it more interesting and funny as hell when I come back to life. We were even thinking of taking bets on how many people faint, scream or whatever when I do get back up."

These guys thought this was hysterical but Tallulah wasn't amused. She thought it was a stupid idea. It was extra nice when she complained that their shenanigans ruined what was supposed to be a relaxing night in with me. She also didn't think the ball players would kill Gus just because he might or might not be a Nazi. "Oh, but I have more than one trick up my sleeve." He took note that he didn't have any sleeves, or any part of a shirt on for that matter. "I keep my tricks in my pocket."

Gus then got out of the car and started walking towards the court. Kovac never stopped smiling. The excitement he displayed at the potential violence of the situation made me think that he probably owned the whole collection of Faces of Death movies and anything remotely like a snuff film.

Just before he got close enough for the players and bystanders to notice him, Gus reached into his "magic pocket" and retrieved his "trick." Tallulah and I couldn't tell what it was until he put it on. Kovac, of course, already knew because he was practically convulsing with laughter now. Where the fuck did Gus get a Ku Klux Klan mask and hood?

Everyone on and around the court just froze in place as Gus walked up to the free-throw line. I couldn't hear him but I'm sure he said something really insulting to the guys standing around. I thought Kovac would have an aneurysm from laughing by this point because Gus was now dancing on the court. As far as dancing goes, I guess he was doing a decent job emulating different popular moves but no one knew what to the think of his performance.

It wasn't until he snatched the basketball away and started dribbling it around the court that anyone appeared to get over being stunned and look visibly upset or bothered. Someone spat at him so Gus kicked the basketball into the night. I have to admit I was pretty impressed with the distance he achieved on that. He must have played soccer in high school.

This pissed off one of the bigger guys, who had probably been the owner of that basketball. He walked up to Gus, who now looked like something out of Adolf Hitler's A Night At The Roxbury. The dancing stopped when the big guy caught Gus in the face with a quick right hook, dropping him to the floor instantly. Everyone held their breath, waiting to see what happened next.

Gus responded immediately by getting up and running towards the parking lot and jumping on the roof of the nicest car there--I believe it was a navy blue Ford Explorer. Could you believe that crazy fuck started pissing on the hood of that car? It's safe to say there wasn't a single person there who didn't want to kill Gus by that point.

After getting dragged off of the car and having the shit beaten out of him, which included getting hit with a garbage can, Gus finally got what he wanted. Someone in that crowd had had enough of his ridiculous intrusion and shot him. We couldn't tell who it was because it was so crowded around Gus but it was definitely three shots and that sent everyone scattering, either on foot or in their cars.

When the place cleared out, all that was left was Gus, lying on the floor with his head resting on a pillow of blood. I give him credit for managing to keep that stupid mask and hood on throughout the whole thing. We waited and after a couple of minutes he slowly sat up and looked around to see no one was there to react to his resurrection. "Fuck you! I'm alive!" I'm sure some of the people who left on foot heard him yell that.

He was laughing and still wearing his get up when he got into the car. It had three bullet holes where his face and forehead would be. Tallulah was the one who angrily pulled it off of him. "What the fuck is wrong with you?! Do you realize how dumb that was?" He didn't see what the big deal was.

"Maybe our condition is a fucking blast for you but it's not for me. The only time I feel any kind of happiness is when I'm dying and I think 'maybe this is finally it.' But I'm not gonna make a sick game out of it to traumatize people by exploiting the fact we don't stay fucking dead." I was kind of hurt by Tallulah's words but I didn't say anything. I thought all the time she spent with me, regardless if I killed her or not, made her happy but I was just being

156

sensitive. She had to enjoy our time together. If she didn't then she deserves an award for acting. I'm not going to read into it...that much.

The rest of the ride consisted of her scolding Gus and Kovac, who couldn't stop laughing, about exposing their ability to outsiders. The fact that Tallulah had brought me into this group made me think of The Lost Boys. I was Michael and Tallulah was Star. She had drawn me into her coven of vampires and I would either become one of them or die because they never exposed their true selves to anyone unless they were about to kill them or make them join up. I'm just glad I met Tallulah at the factory and not where Michael meets Star. I'd never be caught at an outdoor concert where some oiled up, body building, Mad Max extra with a saxophone is headlining.

It was cool at the time though, huh?

We got back to Tallulah's and she stood in her doorway for a few minutes while Gus apologized and explained that he wasn't a racist. I believed that he wasn't a racist. It didn't suit him and he thought it was a stupid thing to be since bloodlines were all over the place and who gives a shit what nationality you are. Gus only had two categories of people: Interesting and uninteresting. Most people he would say fall under the uninteresting banner.

Tallulah didn't believe he was a racist either. She was just mad that they dragged us along for something they should have known she wouldn't approve of. "I'm really sorry, okay? I thought it would be funny to fuck with the locals and make them think they killed someone. I guess I just like to piss people off."

"Well, you succeeded", was Tallulah's response right before she slammed her door in Gus and Kovac's faces. We could hear the tires of Kovac's Barracuda screeching away from the house in protest. They were probably fairly upset about getting chewed out but fuck'em, they shouldn't have included us. Tallulah sat next to me on the couch, laying her head on my shoulder. I hadn't noticed how tired she looked. Perhaps the events of the evening had drained her energy. I know my battery was next to empty.

As she fell asleep, she whispered, "They could have gotten you killed, Guy. That's not how it's supposed to happen. So careless..." And like that, she was fast asleep. I didn't want to move her or leave so I just closed my eyes until I fell asleep too.

I dreamed I was floating through the clouds, high above open plains and hills. The sky was completely red. I couldn't see myself, only what my eyes were seeing. There didn't seem to be anyone left in the world. There was no sound either, just some faint music in the distance but I couldn't make it out.

There was a sense of freedom at first but the longer I floated the less in control I felt. Soon it was like I was being drawn to something terrible against my will. Something bad was happening and there was nothing I could do about it. I just kept floating, closer and closer to this awful thing there was no way of preventing.

I don't remember much more than that and when I woke up, Tallulah was still lying on me, asleep. She had tears rolling down her face. Later, when she drifted awake, she just looked at me and smiled. I wanted to ask her what she dreamt about but for some reason I felt it was best not to. For now anyways.

158

THE FUNERAL PORTRAIT

Feeling Very Strange Today,

Guy

JUNE 20TH

To My Dear Family,

Back to business as usual. I killed Tallulah this week a total of four times. I ran her over with my car. That felt way worse than the couple of times I've run over a possum or raccoon in the road. You can't help but feel your heart stop for that second when your car suddenly hits a bump that is not supposed to be there. Even if you see that bump waving at you and lying in the road beforehand.

Another time, in Tallulah's living room, I filled her mouth with broken glass and tied a noose around her neck. She hung above the couch, tearing up her throat and mouth with the glass as she struggled to suck in air. It looked like a Dario Argento movie.

I sat and waited for her return, thumbing through a magazine. I noticed an ad for cell phones and thought one of them resembled the phone she had broken that time she fell off the factory roof. I must've been thinking out loud because a second later, while still dangling above, she used one of her toes to point out the correct one. We could have done without the broken glass. I think she's still finding little fragments of it in her mouth. I really screwed myself over on that one if you know what I mean. You probably do, Bruno.

The pressure was on so I thought really hard about something she hadn't tried yet. This led us to the food market, where I picked up a few sirloin steaks. Then we drove over to this junkyard I've passed a few times while picking up a body. I always noticed when driving by that there were two mean as Hell looking Rottweilers guarding the place. The kind of dogs that could chew paint off the walls.

After locating the best spot to hop over the fence, I tied the steaks to Tallulah near her major arteries and gave her a boost into the junkyard. Those dogs were on her in seconds. The steaks were gone in the blink of an eye and then they went to town on Tallulah. Now, if I was a crazed, flesh-eating dog I'd be pretty excited too about a hot chick jumping over my fence in the middle of the night. I threw some extra steaks away from her body to distract them so she could heal.

I only wish I had a video camera to record how funny she looked when she came back to life and had about a five-second window to get up and get her ass back over the fence before the dogs tore her apart again. What was left of her dress got caught on the metal wiring and stayed put as the rest of her fell to the ground on my side. Even she couldn't stop laughing at how ridiculous she looked tumbling down in only a blood soaked bra and panties.

For the last kill, I couldn't really think of anything great so I just snuck up behind her while she watched television and broke her neck. I didn't even think that would actually work. They make it look so easy in action movies but I had to really use a lot of force and jerk her head back and forth a couple of time before I heard the snap.

She was so impressed and turned on by the strength and brute force I displayed in doing this that I couldn't keep her off of me for the rest of the night. Thank God she finally got out all of those pieces of glass in her mouth or I would be walking in a really funny manner today.

I'd like to say I'm getting good at this but she's still alive. I'm starting to feel like a serial killer who only goes after the same victim over and over and over.

I Swear I'm Not A Serial Killer,

Guy

JUNE 21ST

To My Dear Family,

Tallulah had an idea today that I really liked. She mentioned how we had spent all this time together but didn't have one single picture to prove it. I asked her what she wanted to do about that and she told me to go by her house and to wear the black suit that I use at work during memorial services.

There was a note on the front door letting me know it was unlocked. I let myself in and saw that she had candles going all over the place. Some people might have found it creepy if they were coming over for the first time but I knew a romantic gesture from Tallulah when I saw one. "What a lucky girl I am to have the most handsome man in Florida standing in my living room."

She was at the top of the stairs and it was a moment I could never forget in a million years. The array of candles created a soft, shadowy light that danced across her smooth, pale face as they flickered. Her full lips were a dark shade of red lipstick I had yet to see her wear. The black makeup around her eyes made them all the more otherworldly than they usually were. And the dress she had on...words don't exist that would properly describe how amazing she looked in this long black and red number.

The fiery red she always dyed her hair was fresh and glistening. Tallulah had it pulled back tightly with a part on one side. The rest of it was securely fastened in a bun, behind her head. This showed off her long, succulent neck that was every vampire's fantasy. On either side, hung matching black earrings that brought such an elegant touch to her ensemble. I didn't even notice I had been holding my breath while taking in the image of this...she is the most beautiful woman to ever walk this Earth. Ever.

In my life I have seen breath-taking sunsets that only the great Artist in the Heavens could have created. I've listened to brilliantly written music that couldn't have been composed by anyone short of genius. I've viewed paintings so rich in color and detail it's as if life itself took residence in their canvases. I've read words so eloquently strung together they rose from the page and wrapped themselves around my very soul.

But all of the world's magnificence went up in flames in Tallulah's presence. There simply wasn't enough beauty for her and anything else. She embodied it all. The most gorgeous flowers imaginable would be honored to be given to her.

Like a Siren she lured me up the stairs and took my hand. I would have followed her anywhere at that moment, even to my death. Tallulah only wanted to go to her bedroom, however. I hadn't been in there since my first visit when I woke up in the casket. We'd been utilizing the normal guest bedroom this whole time.

Her room was exactly how I remembered it, only there was now a chair by the casket and an old-style camera, set up on a tripod nearby. "I want us to take a Funeral Portrait, Guy." I knew exactly what she meant. Years ago, people used to pose for pictures with the body or bodies of loved ones as they laid in either, a casket, bed or seat of some sort. Photographs were so expensive that this was often the only opportunity a family had to take a picture with that particular person. It wasn't considered uncommon, strange or even a frightening thing. It was just a way of remembering someone that was important to you. People don't do it so much today but it still happens. We all grieve differently.

I picked up Tallulah and carefully placed her in the casket. She got situated while I made sure the camera had us in full view. "I want it to look authentic that's why I'm not using a digital camera. And the film stock is black and white, of course." Of course.

The camera was ready to go. I handed her a bouquet she had on the dresser. I set the timer and took the seat beside her. She lay there with her eyes closed, clutching the bouquet to her stomach. On my best day I'd never be able to present a more exquisite corpse. Three seconds later, while doing my best to look relaxed and emotionless, the camera flashed and captured our Funeral Portrait.

Tallulah didn't budge until I leaned over and kissed her lips. A sly grin took form in her face and she opened her eyes. "I just knew someday my Prince would come and awaken me from my slumber with his kiss." What dost thou Sleeping Beauty wish of thy Prince now that she has risen from the very slumber she speaks of? "She would love for you to help her out this coffin. Sleeping Beauty really has to pee." Done.

After Tallulah went to the little girl's room we took a drive to the old glass factory. She had made a nice picnic basket for us and we ate our dinner on the roof. We even had a bottle of champagne and music. (I bought her a new radio after using the previous one to electrocute her in the bathtub that time.)

It was a full moon last night and every star in the sky seemed to have come out to join us. We found a classical station and waltzed for a bit. I was proud of the fact I didn't step on her toes not once. Then I sat Tallulah on the railing, facing me, so we could talk.

"I'll develop our picture tomorrow. I think it's going to come out great."

Yeah, me too. And you know, I think I'm really starting to enjoy trying to kill you.

"Yes, well don't get too used to it. I would like to die sometime soon if that's all right with you." (chuckle)

You know, Tallulah, I don't think I've ever told you what truly beautiful eyes you have.

"Oh, go on."

No, I'm serious. They have so much character and depth. Looking into them I can tell you've seen a lot.

"I have." (awkward silence)

What do you see right now?

"Hmmm... I see what is easily the most beautiful person I have ever known, who is also the one person in the whole world who I think has any idea what it's like being me."

Well, that's easily the nicest thing anyone has ever said to me.

"It's easy to say nice things to you."

She leaned in and gave me such a sweet kiss. It intensified the effects of the champagne, which already had me a little light headed. Then a new piece of music came on the radio and Tallulah gasped. I automatically thought something terrible was about to happen but she told me she was excited because the most beautiful song ever written was playing. It was a sign that her and I were destined to meet and help each other, she said.

The song that came on was an aria named "When I Am Laid In Earth" from Henry Purcell's tragic opera, Dido and Aeneas. Tallulah said most people--herself included--just called it, "Dido's Lament." Dido, the Queen of Carthage, falls in love with the Trojan, Aeneas. However, they are pulled apart through the conniving acts of a Sorceress and Dido is left alone to wallow in her sadness. She in turn decides she cannot go on living with such heartbreak.

> When I am laid, am laid in earth, May my wrongs create
> No trouble, no trouble in thy breast;
> Remember me, remember me, but ah! forget my fate.
> Remember me, but ah! forget my fate.

It was the most emotional piece of music I have ever heard. It made my eyes water. Tallulah wasn't able to fight off her tears though as we listened to the lovely, mournful words come forth in such powerful singing. As the music finished out the lament we kissed more passionately than we ever had.

When our lips separated and our eyes stared miles into each other I wanted so badly to do something to show Tallulah how much I cared. Something to prove to her how serious I was about making her happy. I needed to show her how much she meant to me. I could think of only one thing to do at that moment that would convey my devotion to her.

I pushed her off the roof.

She didn't die but it was the thought that counts she said. I packed up all of our stuff and met her by where she landed. I got another big smooch for my efforts and spent the rest of the night making love to the most amazing woman in the entire world.

You would disagree with me Bruno because you love fake tits. I don't doubt you'd find Tallulah hot but without a plastic chest she wouldn't crack your top ten. Make no mistake though--she IS the hottest thing since the sun. And she orbits the planet Guy on a daily basis.

Sometimes life is actually good,

Guy

HOW MUCH CAN ONE PERSON SUFFER?

JUNE 24TH

Dear Guy,

I know I've asked a lot of you. And I know you feel like what I want is murder. I've tried my best to convince you that you're simply euthanizing me but it's not exactly like putting a dog to sleep, is it? Up to now, I've been pretty secretive with my background and for good reason. When you're someone who can't die but wants to, it's not very smart to revisit the memories that made life so worthless to you in the first place.

You seem to think I'm this strong woman who has stared Hell in the face on a regular basis and soldiers on, but the truth is, what choice do I have? I

169

may be desensitized to the blood and horror of my daily suicides but the pain that inspires them is very much intact. I've had no reason to live for years and years and therein, I believe, lies my problem.

It's like a suicide bomber. How can you possibly dissuade them if the worst thing you can threaten them with is death? How can I end my life when not one ounce of me cares about the consequences of suicide? Not only for me, but for anyone who may know me. Even the most depressed people who kill themselves might have had a shred of guilt over what they were doing towards the end. The pain could be too much to bear and suicide is the only way out but what about that nephew in Massachusetts? Or that estranged brother in New York? They didn't know you felt this way. How will they feel when they find out you didn't love them enough to stick around or seek out their help?

Not everyone thinks that way of course. When you get to that point, you're not thinking of other people. All you can think about is how much you want the pain to go away. Maybe you think of other people when you're standing out on the ledge and that's what stops you. That's not a bad thing. You are much nicer and less selfish than I am. That's probably because you have had a considerably happier life than me. I don't say that to trivialize your depression. I say that only as a possible explanation for your inability to successfully commit suicide. Again, not being able to kill yourself (in your case) is not a bad thing. There is still hope for you. My hope died a long time ago and my body is just trying to catch up.

Welcome to my nightmare.

THE FUNERAL PORTRAIT

Don't say I didn't warn you,

Tallulah

JUNE 25TH

Dear Guy,

I can't tell you the exact moment I first wanted to die, because I don't remember, but I do know my problems started when I was nine years old. Some girls at school had been bullying me that year but I never said anything because I figured they would stop eventually. They didn't.

On one occasion they followed me into the restroom during lunch. My bladder was on the verge of bursting but they wouldn't let me pee. I tried to fight them off but when it's three against one and you're small like I was, it's a losing battle. A combination of the ridicule and the pain from having to use the toilet forced me to start crying.

The evil, little future whores started calling me a baby and told me to stand in the corner, sucking my thumb or they would all smack me in the face really hard. I did as I was told in the hopes of being rid of them. They all took turns smacking me anyway. I wasn't allowed to stop sucking my thumb either as this went on.

When they got bored with the slapping they resorted to pulling my hair. They were really determined to actually pull some of my hair out so they gave it quick, hard yanks which hurt like you wouldn't believe but I guess they

172

weren't strong enough to get more than a few hairs at a time. That was enough to cause some bleeding on my scalp but it was mostly hidden by the rest of the hair they couldn't rip from my head.

Finally, driven by the desire to end things with a bang, the biggest of the three told me to stand with my legs spread apart. Still sucking my thumb, face pulsating and red, not to mention stinging from my tears, I again did as I was told. Even as she prepared herself I couldn't figure out what she was planning to do. A few seconds later that fucking bitch kicked me in the crotch so hard my insides shook.

What kind of little girl kicks another little girl in the crotch? She may have only been nine, but her sneaker hit with so much force, I'm guessing if you kicked a football the exact same way, you'd be looking at a fifty-five yard field goal, at least.

My crying intensified, which made me start gagging. It hurt so much that I didn't even realize I had started peeing on myself until one of them pointed it out with laughter. I was so embarrassed, Guy. All I wanted was someone to come through the door and save me but no one came. That was the first time I felt completely alone and helpless.

I ended up hiding in the restroom for the remainder of the day and snuck out as soon as the last bell rang. I also came down with a mysterious "illness" that kept me out of school the rest of the week.

Naturally, all my time at school was spent wondering what new torment I would be subjected to by my "admirers." My grades, which had always been

173

excellent, were dropping drastically. The smart thing would've been to tell someone about these bullies but I was too scared of further provoking them.

My parents noticed my schoolwork slipping, particularly my father, Rupert. He and my mother, Miriam, got into a vicious fight about it one night. My dad wasn't necessarily a bad man, just a bitter one. His story was a common one. Star of the high school football team, dating the prettiest girl in school (my mom.) After graduation he chose the Army over college and marriage. My mom decided to wait for him and she didn't have to wait very long. After only a month overseas, he was wounded in combat (took two bullets in the back, one in the leg) and was honorably discharged from the service.

My mom took this as a sign that they were meant to be together. The way she saw it, those three bullets saved his life. He didn't feel that way. When he got home, he had returned as a failure in his eyes. A couple of schools still would've been willing to offer him a football scholarship but his injuries made it impossible for him to perform anywhere near the caliber he was used to. So no military. No college. All that was left was marriage.

He and my mother would be married for almost ten years before I came along. That was unlucky for me because by then they could barely stand each other. How they managed to have the sex necessary to produce me is a mystery. And trust me, I've looked into it, I'm definitely theirs.

My father was convinced my bad grades were just the beginning and if I wasn't disciplined immediately I would end up throwing my life away. My mother on the other hand didn't think a couple of F's were the end of the world. She figured I would do better during the next marking period.

Dad--I'll just call them Mom and Dad so it simplifies things--Dad hated when Mom treated him like he was overreacting or made him out to be the bad guy. He just wanted me to get my act together before it was too late but Mom--as she always did--accused him of being way too dramatic.

This one night Dad had had one too many drinks so his usual patience was long gone. He got physical right away. Most of the time, Mom, had to really get under his skin to earn a smack or something equally nasty. Dad grabbed her by the arm in a manner that probably would have dislocated my shoulder at that age.

"You know, I'm getting a little fucking tired of you disrespecting me, Miriam. Is this how you want to teach our daughter to treat me? Like I'm a fucking joke?" She ignored his question and instead told him that he was hurting her arm.

"Answer me, goddamnit! Do you think I'm a joke?!" In the most sarcastic tone I can remember ever coming from her, Mom told him, "Yes, Rupert. You're hysterical. In fact, I think you get even funnier with every beer you drink." Only Mom never got to finish that last word. Dad's fist cut her off with a powerful right hook to the face. Mom flew back, falling over a chair and hitting the kitchen table on the way down. He was a long way from being fit for the military or football but Dad was definitely still strong enough to beat the shit out of someone--especially a woman.

Neither of them noticed that I was standing there the whole time. I was nailed to the spot. I didn't even dare take a breath as all this unfolded. Even to this day I constantly replay that image of Mom stumbling over the chair and table as she falls down. She struggles to get back on her feet right away but her eyes keep rolling back, fighting off a possible concussion. Steam is practically rising from Dad's head as he stands over her, fist clenched as if debating whether she needs another one for good measure.

Mom did manage to get up fairly quickly and in relative silence as if trying to not further draw attention, despite Dad staring her down the entire time. Her eyes were already red and tearing but I could tell she was doing her best to not burst out crying. The punch must've hurt because the left side of her face was already swollen and bruised like a scraped knee. Dad slowly turned to me and our eyes locked with each other. Remorse and extreme hatred seemed to be fighting for control of his expression in a look of ambivalence that still haunts me. This was all because of me and my stupid F's.

Mom said she was going for a walk. That's what she did whenever her and Dad fought--go for a walk--even if it was only a battle of words. She almost knocked me over as she walked passed. I don't know if she did this on purpose because it was mostly my fault that she got punched or if she was just so frightened and wanting to get the hell out of there so fast that she didn't even notice me. I think it's because she didn't see me. How could she with one eye swollen shut and the other being a blurry mess of tears?

Dad kept staring at me with that same twisted expression until the door slammed shut behind us. He put his head down and slowly walked away. I used the opportunity to run over to the window just in time to see Mom disappear into the darkness of the street outside as she did her own walking away. That was the last time I saw her alive.

No one would tell me exactly what happened, but I overheard a couple of cops talking about what, whoever she ran into that night, did to her. I can barely think it, let alone write it down, so you'll just have to take my word for it that it was a horrible fate no one deserves. If there's any fairness, at all, in this world, she died quickly.

Over the next couple of years my grades got worse as did Dad's drinking, but he didn't care about much of anything anymore. He would often come home with hookers or even runaway teens willing to have sex for some cash and a place to stay that night. Anything to not go to sleep alone.

I was only eleven years old but I knew what was going on and I hated it. Almost every night I would be in the living room watching television and Dad would come home with one of his "disposable girlfriends" I called them. Sometimes he came home when I was already in bed, but I tried to stay up as late as I could. For some reason I felt like I had to see these women he was bringing into our house. More importantly, I wanted them to see me. I wanted them to feel ashamed for what they were doing. I wanted them to feel like shit for not being Mom. I wanted Dad to see my disapproval. Even at that age I could stare daggers like you wouldn't believe.

So one night Dad comes home with this skinny redhead, who was wearing a month's supply of makeup. I would later find out she was only fourteen. I gave them my usual angry look and they quickly retreated to the bedroom. I had to raise the volume on the television twice to drown out the sounds of them having sex. That always made me sick to my stomach.

I finally decided to go to bed and turned off the television when I heard all this commotion from the bedroom. Suddenly, there came the most eerie, heart-pounding silence I've ever experienced.

I carefully crept into Dad's bedroom and I found him sitting on the floor, completely naked and covered in blood. There was a hammer next to him, which I'll never forget had a clump of red hair still stuck to it. On the bed, the girl he had brought home was very much dead and laying in a mess of her own blood and skull bits. He had to have brought the hammer down several times to do that kind of damage. I began to hyperventilate with panic when Dad looked up at me.

He was crying out of these empty eyes I never imagined belonging to my father. "You don't know what it's like, baby. You don't know what it's like to be this sad. You don't know my pain."

I didn't know what to do but stand there, silently crying. Dad started weeping loudly which turned into uncontrollable sobbing. I had no idea what I could possibly do for him so I just backed out of the room and closed the door. All I wanted to do was throw myself onto my bed and cry until I realized that this was all a dream. I was even willing to accept Mom's death if only what had just happened was a dream.

Not more than a minute later, a single gunshot interrupted my praying that the horrors of Dad's bedroom were untrue. I don't have to tell you where

178

that bullet ended up. I would go the next three years without saying one word. The police never figured out Dad's motive for killing that girl. Neither did I for that matter. I'm guessing his mind just finally snapped. I give him credit for lasting as long as he did.

The next five years were mostly spent in a group home. They tried putting me in foster homes a couple of times but it didn't take. My not talking or even acknowledging most people didn't go over well. And my only relative was the uncle I told you about, who left me all that money. They couldn't get a hold of him and besides, after finding out the type of lifestyle he had, I doubt they would have let me live with him for long.

I was now a ward of the state and would in all likelihood live out the rest of my childhood in this group home with the other castaways. Everyone thought I was a mute at first. Obviously I can talk--it's just that I didn't have it in me to say anything at the time. No words could express how I felt so I figured why bother.

When I was sixteen I met my first love at that very same group home. His name was Brandon. He was a strong, handsome boy who was really sweet for a little while but a tad too frisky. He would ask me, "Are you ready, Tallulah?" And when I asked what I should be ready for, he would always respond, "I wanna fuck." A real ladies man, that Brandon.

I enjoyed kissing him a lot. No, not as much as I enjoy kissing you, so don't get all jealous on me, big boy. I know how you are.

After a couple of months of seeing each other, we pretty much had this exchange every day, which always ended in Brandon storming off and ignoring me. Like I said, I enjoyed the kissing and didn't even mind how much his hands explored but I was only sixteen and I wanted my first time to be romantic. He would say, "But I'm horny!" As if I would say, "Oh, well why didn't you say so? That makes all the difference. Here, let me just strip myself naked and get on all fours for you. Have at it, cowboy."

Brandon's sweetness was wearing off fast the more I refused to have sex with him. He didn't even want to make out with me as much because he felt that was teasing. One day though he wanted me to sneak off to one of our secret spots with him so we could talk and cuddle, he said. I was excited because I thought he'd gotten over the sex thing and was willing to wait until I felt the moment was right.

His idea of cuddling was grabbing my tits and trying to get me to put my hand down his pants. I was so upset and hurt by this that I shoved him away as hard as I could. He barely budged. Brandon stood there, grinding his teeth and then asked, "Do you trust me, Tallulah?" I tried to tell him that I did, I just wasn't ready for sex. He didn't let me get beyond the words "I do but--" before he knocked the wind out of me with a hard uppercut to my stomach. I started gasping for air, trying not to throw up when he punched me again, this time in the face. In that quick moment, I thought of the night Mom died.

If the punches didn't do the trick, then me breaking my fall with my head did. I lay on the floor, bleeding and disoriented. I could feel him yanking my pants and underwear off of me but was way too out of it to fight him. I knew what was coming and my body had not one bit of strength or coordination to prevent it.

Brandon got on top of me from behind and forced himself into me. I wasn't even sure where he was sticking it at first because the pain was so intense it made everything hurt. I didn't want to further enrage him so I just laid there--crying and wincing in pain as quietly as I could while the first love of my life fucked me like a dead piece of meat. He pulled at my hair a lot, much in the same way those bitches pulled my hair in the girl's bathroom.

He finished off with a few extra hard thrusts and stayed where he was, never pulling out. I prayed that he would get off of me so I could go find a corner somewhere to die in. That's the worst thing you could do to someone, Guy. Taking a person's life is awful if it isn't for a good reason but to completely violate them is worse because they have to go on living with that.

Brandon pulled my hair back again and touched his lips to my ear. I wished I'd never kissed those lips with such passion. I wished I'd never kissed them all. I'm sure at that moment I also wished those lips were lying dead at the bottom of a lake with the rest of his scumbag body. He whispered, "If you tell anyone about this I will fucking kill you. Do you understand?" I told him that I did and my submission must have turned him on because instead of getting off of me, he began round two. Somehow it hurt just as much as the first time around.

Like I said, I don't remember exactly when it was, but I'm sure somewhere around this time was when I first thought about killing myself. I didn't think I could handle the aftermath of being raped the first time. It

181

seemed all the more worse that it was someone whom I loved and trusted that did this to me.

Yes, this wasn't the last time I would be sexually assaulted. I would soon find out the difference between having someone I love rape me and a total stranger doing it. That's not something little girls aspire to accomplish when they grow up. And I really don't have the strength to elaborate right now. But I will.

Are you running, screaming, from me yet?

Tallulah

JUNE 26TH

Dear Guy,

After what happened with Brandon, I knew the group home wasn't safe anymore. I believed him when he said he would kill me if I told anyone what had happened. There wasn't a single trace of the boy I loved in the voice that whispered that to me. Besides, I was practically a woman now, so I decided to run away.

I couldn't have picked a worse day to take off. It was raining--like end of the world rain--and I was out in the pitch black of night, soaked all the way through, trying to hitchhike on a road that would probably be deserted even without the rain or late hour being a factor. At about three o'clock in the morning a dark red pickup truck stopped to give me a ride. It was the only car I had seen all night.

The driver was this grimy looking hillbilly, shit-kicker, with a huge beer belly sticking out of a filthy wife-beater. I instantly knew where he got his gut from because the floor of the car was littered with empty beer cans and junk food wrappers. From the smell of him and his swerving, you could tell he had probably polished the booze off that very evening. I wanted to jump out while he was driving. I should have.

Neither of us had said one word after my initial "thanks" when he picked me up. It was the most awkward silence I've ever known. Maybe ten minutes had passed when I noticed he was undoing his belt and pants. He reached in and pulled out the most disgusting looking penis I've ever seen. Sadly, it was the first I had ever seen at the time, since I never actually saw Brandon's.

I asked him what he was doing and he said, "It's not what I'm doin', lil' lady. It's what you're gonna be doin'." I asked him what he could possibly expect me to do. "You're gonna put this cock in that pretty young mouth of yours and you won't take it out 'til I say so." I couldn't believe what he was saying. I wanted to get out of there so bad but he had increased his speed and if I jumped out, I risked injuring myself badly or worse. He seemed like the type that would stop his car if I bailed, just so he could come run over me as I struggled to get to my feet.

He started laughing at the horrified look on my face. It was a terrible, queasy laugh. He reached out with his free hand and grabbed a fistful of my hair. It's a miracle I have any left since everyone in my life seems to like fucking pulling on it. The Grimy Man shoved my head down into his crotch with a power I didn't expect. He was way stronger than Brandon.

I felt that disgusting thing against my face and I puked all over his lap. He laughed harder and reached out again, touching me everywhere as I tried to block him. This couldn't have been the first time he'd done this because my resistance didn't phase the scumbag. This was all second nature to him.

The group home and even Brandon's violent sexual appetite now seemed like fun. No one could hear me for miles, I was sure of it, but I screamed anyway. I screamed until I saw spots before my eyes. Then the back of his big strong hand came flying at my face and everything went black.

I don't know how much time passed before I slowly drifted awake. My head felt split open, like a thousand migraines rolled into one. My vision was severely blurred but I could kind of make out a dark figure hovering over me. I strained to make out who it was and soon recognized the outline of the Grimy Man. He was on top of me and grunting like a fucking boar.

The pain in my head eased up the tiniest bit. Just enough to realize what was going on. I was being raped again. For the second time in less than a week, some fucking degenerate low-life was having his way with me. I know I must have been completely naked because I could feel his nasty sweat all over me.

The Grimy Man's fat belly pushed down on mine with each painful thrust. He alternated between sucking my breasts and my neck. Both were equally unpleasant. I thought of Brandon and how we had been so happy for a time. He had made love to me compared to what was happening now. All I could do was let my eyes roll back as I lost consciousness again. That was probably the best available option I had at that moment.

For the next eight days I was beaten, starved, raped, burned and sliced. At least that's what I was told. I don't remember much about my ordeal. Doctors said I was severely traumatized and probably repressed the experience to help me get on with my life. I did eventually learn the Grimy Man's real name, but I'd rather not write it down. Please don't ask me to tell you. I've never even spoken about any of this to anyone who wasn't already directly involved, like the police and my doctors at the time.

The group home people had reported me missing but it wasn't me the police were looking for when they kicked in the door. Apparently, the Grimy Man had done this to several other young girls in the area. The trail finally led back to his house.

Luckily, they found him before I was killed. That's what they told me, that I was "lucky." Somehow, "lucky" isn't the word I would choose to describe how I felt when I was rescued.

One of the things I do remember was when the police shot him dead. I was tied to a chair. Aside from a few scraps of torn clothing, I was naked. The Grimy Man had kicked it over on its side, so my face was against the floor. There was all this shouting and commotion and then four or five gunshots later, the Grimy Man fell to the ground, right beside me. Of all that happened since he picked me up in the rain, the thing I will remember most is how I felt seeing him land next to me, looking into my eyes with that dead expression.

Numb.

Sometimes I feel like those dead eyes are still staring at me. Like the Grimy Man is patiently waiting for me to join him the way I was meant to on the floor of his house. I should have died there. I wish I had. I was the victim then.

Now, I'm the worst thing that has ever happened to me.

THE FUNERAL PORTRAIT

It gets worse,

Tallulah

JUNE 27TH

Dear Guy,

I somehow managed to put a few of the shattered pieces back together and go on living my life. I couldn't just break down and be a vegetable for the rest of my days and suicide wasn't a serious option yet, just a sort of morbid fantasy. Optimism wasn't my strongest virtue but I tried to embrace it. I assumed the worst was behind me. I assumed.

Being of age now, I lived on my own and worked to support myself. I had a job at a small bookstore which I really liked because the owner was very nice to me and reading was one of the few things I enjoyed. I even got a say into what type of books we ordered.

It was at this job that I met a guy I would fall in love with. He didn't have one mean bone in his body and he was so sweet to me. It was exactly what I needed. His only problem was he made me seem like Mary Poppins in terms of personality. He was a very depressed young man.

He said to me once, "I don't mean it to sound bad, because I know you've had your problems, but sometimes I envy you. You lost both of your parents when you were young. I had the misfortune of growing up with both of mine. If only people could trade lives like baseball cards."

I don't think he would have enjoyed my life so much if he knew everything I went through after Mom and Dad were gone. He really was the nicest guy. I hoped that our love would bring him out of his depression eventually. I thought if I showed him that life was worth living that kind of thinking would rub off on him.

Despite our love, he hung himself in his bathroom after visiting his parents one afternoon. I went over to his apartment to try and cheer him up. We talked for a little while and watched some TV. I thought he'd be all right, but then he excused himself to the bathroom. After a few minutes I got concerned and went to check on him. He was already dead when I found him. A note by the sink read only, "I'm sorry."

As if the God's of Misery hadn't already rained a shit storm down on my parade, the next two boyfriends I had after that committed suicide as well. One overdosed on heroin and the other threw himself off of a bridge, falling onto a busy highway. I had hoped the overdose was an accident but he'd left a note confirming his intentions.

It had to be me. Oh, I'll admit that all of these guys were not the most joyful people when I met them but something about me gave them the will to give up. Each time, aside from the general depression they suffered, everything was going well with our relationship so their deaths were always a surprise.

I told myself that was it after the bridge jumper. I wasn't going to add to Tallulah's Bermuda Triangle of Despair, as I called it. Three people had decided my love wasn't worth sticking around for. Four if you count my Dad.

I guess I've always been attracted to guys with issues. (As you can see not much has changed.) All I wanted to do though was love and be loved. I don't think I really did anything to push these men over the edge; definitely not on purpose. Sometimes I feel like if I had left them alone to wallow in their own despondency, they'd still be alive--miserable but alive. Somehow, I gave them the inspiration to die but I don't know how. Now I don't even know how to die myself. You add all this together, combined with the usual stressful bullshit life deals everyone and you've got yourself one seriously fucked up chick.

Not much of a life, huh? Shit, I wouldn't even call it a life. It's Hell... and I don't want it anymore.

Help me,
Tallulah

SOMEONE ELSE'S PAIN

JUNE 30TH

To My Dear Family,

Tallulah gave me this diary to read, to better understand her. At least she hopes it will help me better understand her. She told me on the surface it was a typical diary, written by a typical mental patient with a typical outlook on his situation. But below the surface there was what he was really trying to say and it couldn't be more different from what was up front. She told me if I could read between the lies then I'd be able to read between the lines too and see what this person is actually trying to convey to whoever may read their words. It also seems like they wrote it as a last minute, desperate attempt to leave some evidence of their existence because there is only writing in a handful of pages and the rest is blank.

Tallulah tells me that diaries aren't for writing down how well everything is going, unless things were previously really bad and you need to see on paper that they've gotten better. No one fills a diary with just happy thoughts, unless they are a very young girl writing about who she has a crush on and how many dolls she owns. Diaries are for your troubles, which is why most people seem crazy in them. It's a way to get all the bad shit out of your system or at least to make note of it.

I think I know what she means because when I wrote all that crappy poetry back in high school that you guys used to like (minus you, Bruno)--I only did that when I was down. Even if I was writing about something that made me happy, I could only do so when I was depressed. Well, one of my teachers read through my poetry book and wanted to know if I had problems at home or if I needed to speak to a "professional." At the time, I was like, "What the fuck are you talking about?" I can see now why they thought that. That teacher could only see what I was saying on top. They couldn't really tell what I was talking about. This I know for a fact, because the poem they found the most disturbing was the one I wrote about how much I loved paper airplanes. That idiot completely misinterpreted my symbolism.

And for the record, I don't think it's unheard of to keep a record of your daily experiences, whether they are good or bad. I mean, that's kind of what I'm doing, isn't it? This started out as a suicide letter. It's now turned into a journal of sorts. I was kind of hoping each letter I wrote would replace the previous one so my decision to kill myself would be as clear to you as possible. I guess you'll have a lot more reading to do when I'm gone. Sorry about that.

So Tallulah gave me the diary of someone named Ronald Sykes. She found it on the side of the road a couple of years ago where it looked like someone had tossed it from a moving car. Gus and Kovac have read it as well. They all got the same message from the diary. When I shared my thoughts on it with Tallulah I found that I also got the same thing from it. This made Tallulah happy because she felt this would help me realize what a person shows you can often be the complete opposite of what's inside. I didn't need the diary to know that. Her goal is to make me understand that although she may seem happy when we're together, she is really a car wreck inside beyond repair. I think she believes that if I can accept this then the feelings I have for her will just go away. I don't care how fucked up she is inside. If there's something there at all I'm going to fight for it. That's what I really got from the diary. No matter the odds, if you believe in something, you never give up.

Sykes was very young, perhaps no older than eighteen or so and had been committed to a mental institution. He wrote about his descent into madness and how his condition was treated. The writing has an eerie optimism when discussing Ronald's mental state and the people who helped make him what he is. Tallulah said it didn't take her long to realize everything he was saying was bullshit. All of it was lies and only the right kind of eyes, the kind her, Gus, Kovac and I possessed, could really "see" Ronald Sykes' words. I copied some of his diary for you to read.

What kind of eyes do you have?

VINCENT VIÑAS

Guy

OCTOBER 3RD

(This is what was really written in the diary)

My name is Ronald Sykes. I'm a patient here at Carpenter Hill Sanitarium. If you are reading this book, I probably forgot to take it with me after getting better and going home. That's quite all right because my story may be able to help you realize your goal of complete mental health as well. For awhile I used to be very ill and often found myself in the embarrassing situation of not remembering periods of time. It was during those lost periods of time that my mental illness flourished. I would wake up in the oddest of places, overcome with confusion and have no clue as to how I arrived there. At school I would get into all sorts of trouble for babbling nonsense for hours on end. I'd get into one of my spells and the teacher would calmly escort me to the nurse's office where she and an assistant would place a wet washcloth on my neck to soothe me. Then they'd make me lie down and rest so I wouldn't upset the devils of unreason they said were corrupting my mind.

After all, I was just a young man and wasn't equipped with the necessary tools to battle these demons on my own. I am forever grateful for everything they've done for me.

I guess you can say my mind started deteriorating when I was in grade school. I remember this day in kindergarten when it was nap time and I wasn't tired. All the other children were laid out on blankets and pillows, but I was not sleepy at all. Which was odd because we always had nap time in the afternoon and I always fell asleep. So this one time I told my teacher that I wasn't sleepy and didn't want to take a nap. She insisted that I do and I made a little fuss about it, until she smiled at me and took me by the hand. We quietly walked over to her office just outside the room because the lights were dim for the other napping kids and her office was brighter. She sat me down on just about the most comfy chair I've ever sat in and began explaining to me the need for nap time. With a comforting hand on my shoulder she told me how a growing child needs their rest in order to grow strong. If I didn't nap then I would fall asleep much too early in the evening causing me to awaken much too early as well. Eventually, my body clock would be so thrown off that I would burn myself out.

THE FUNERAL PORTRAIT

I was hoping she would take even longer to explain all this because that chair was so darn comfy. I really had to make a number one though so she took me to the restroom and waited outside while I went. Then we went back to her office where she sang me the sweetest lullaby to make me sleepy. It worked like a charm and in a couple of minutes I was so drowsy she had to carry me back to the classroom. The next thing I remember was waking up feeling like a million bucks and completely convinced that nap time was essential to a healthy lifestyle as far as five-year-olds go. And my teacher told me on my way out of class that if I partook in nap time on a regular basis like the other kids she'd not only keep our little chat a secret from my folks she would also let me take home Flash, the class gerbil, for the weekend. I couldn't stop smiling on the bus going home.

I maintained this special bond with my teacher all through the year. When the other kids were distracted finger painting or napping she would pull me aside and say such encouraging things like "You are such a wonderful little boy, Ronald. When I see you, my face just lights up at the thought of having such an amazing kid in my class. It's an honor to prepare you for what will no doubt be a very bright future." As you can imagine I spent that whole school year loving every minute of it. It was everything I had hoped school would be when I was four. Aside from Ms. Lawler, I made plenty of other friends that year.

My life continued to flourish all through High School. I was always picked first for teams in gym, was very popular with the ladies, had an amazing entourage of friends and had straight A's across the board. My essays always got the highest marks because teachers praised my attention to format and practical approach when it came to expressing myself. They would often put my essays in one of the hallway display cases so whenever they passed it by they knew that my generation would be in good hands.

I loved my teachers. I would get into these incredible debates with them all the time. We would discuss all areas of life. I especially earned some praise from them with my views on politics and how conservative thinking was the only way to maintain values and secure a stronger society. In the end, their intelligence was just too much for my young intellect and I didn't mind telling them so.

I was first brought here to Carpenter Hill Sanitarium five years ago, just prior to my eighteenth birthday. My parents, God Bless them, felt that if I was going to begin my adult life, I should be as healthy as possible— physically and mentally. It was early in the morning on a beautiful June day when the attendants came to pick me up. One of them helped with my luggage as the other escorted me to their vehicle. I hugged and kissed my parents and thanked them for what they were doing for me. It let me know how much they cared. They waved to me as we drove away.

THE FUNERAL PORTRAIT

Since I've been here, several doctors have treated me. Each one has been even nicer than the last. Unfortunately, one of them had to hastily leave his position after becoming very ill. Too bad. He was one of my favorites. And the attendants—you couldn't ask for a better group of people. Sweethearts, every last one of them.

You have to remember when you're in a place like Carpenter Hill, there is nothing the staff wants more than to see you get better and live a healthy mental life. They will stop at nothing until you are of strong mind. For instance, we were having group therapy once and I didn't feel like adding anything to the conversation, being shy and all. So the doctor cleverly got me to talk by asking me questions about stuff I like. I got so into it, I was compelled to stand before the group and further discuss all of my winning qualities that would eventually help me leave Carpenter Hill as a new man. A better man.

I especially love how positive the whole staff is. They're constantly reminding you how important you are and how with their sincere care every single one of us will soon walk out of Carpenter Hill to take our rightful places in society and make it a better place for everyone. I'm so happy to be here. I can't imagine the man I would be if not for being welcomed to this fine establishment. Here, there is always hope and that makes life simply wonderful.

Oh, I believe I hear someone coming. It must be time for my medication. We get our medication and then we watch a movie. I wonder what it will be today. Last time we watched The Wizard of Oz.

Remember what I said. There's always hope at Carpenter Hill. Don't give up. Let them help you and live your life happily knowing <u>they</u> did <u>that</u> for <u>you</u>.

All the best,

Ronald

(This is what I really saw when I read the diary)

I'm Ronnie Sykes. I'm trapped here in Carpenter Hell Nuthouse. If you're reading this it most likely means I'm fucking dead. I've been trying to escape for years and these bastards have probably had enough of my shit. Just follow the worst of many bad smells here and I'm sure you will find me rotting within one of the walls. Don't end up like me. For God's sake, I beg you. Run. I used to always speak my mind and often was ridiculed for having my own thoughts and opinions on the world. Even my family couldn't deal with the fact I wasn't a sheep like them. My parents made a habit out of poisoning me if they were to have company. Sometimes they made me sick. Other times they would sedate me for up to a couple of days. This way no one suspected them of having a free thinking son.

It was the same at school whenever I questioned one of our "lessons." I'd start debating something those asshole teachers would say and suddenly they'd start whipping me with a stick, while a classmate ran for security. They'd drag me, kicking and screaming, to the boiler room and throw me to the floor. If I was lucky the guards just beat the shit out of me. On special occasions they'd rip my clothes off and fuck some sense into me as they called it. I was just a kid. A fucking child who was no match for their strength or determination to ensure that I suffer, physically and mentally--especially physically. Dead or alive, I swear I will forever fucking hate them for what they've done to me.

I was barely out of diapers when I supposedly started going fucking nuts. At least that's what the doctors say. This one time in kindergarten, when they drugged us with milk, I hadn't drank mine and was wide awake. All the little shitheads were on their blankies and baby pillows, but I wanted none of it. I didn't trust sleeping amongst strangers at all. I had been faking it for the first two months of school and couldn't anymore. So I told that bitch, Ms. Lawler, I wasn't going to take naps anymore because it just didn't feel right. She whispered "go to sleep you little fuck" but I just stared at her with confusion. This pissed her off and she immediately scowled at me and yanked my arm. Covering my mouth she carried me out to the hall and shoved me into the janitor's closest because it was really dark in there and out of earshot of the napping kids. There was a portable radiator in there that she plugged in and turned on full blast. She made me sit on it despite the fact it started to cook my ass on contact. What a goddamn bitch. Holding me by my shirt in her angry fist she proceeded to tell me what a bastard I am and how my parents probably wished I was stillborn. I didn't know what the fuck stillborn meant but it didn't sound good.

Then the lousy cunt of a human told me if I didn't take a nap my pee-pee would rot off, eventually falling into the toilet where my parents would flush it down never to be seen again. At that age I was surprised at how well I handled her shit talking but I wished she would hurry the inquisition along because that radiator was murder. She finally let me stand up when I mentioned how much I had to pee. She didn't take me to the restroom though. Instead she demanded that I piss my pants, which at that point wasn't really by choice. Finally, she made me stand still, eyes closed while she spat in my face continuously. I couldn't even react to it. I just had to stand motionless while phlegm from the deepest regions of her cock sucking throat found its way onto my five-year-old face. After wiping my face with my shirt we went back to the classroom where she shoved me to the floor and whispered harshly "now get to fuckin' napping!" A normal kid would have been so scared he would've added a pile of dung to the piss in his undies at that point and force himself to sleep. I just couldn't do it. Defiant little fuck that I was. Am. I did know that I couldn't tell anyone though. That bitch told me that if I told she'd decapitate the class gerbil, Flash, and say I did it. What an evil whore. I couldn't stop crying on the bus going home.

I spent the rest of the school year being tortured by that fucking soulless whore. She never let an opportunity go by to pull me aside when the other little brats were busy and say such horrible things like, "You are such a worthless, little piece of shit, Ronnie. When I just think of you I wanna puke all over the fucking place. That stupid face of yours ruins more days than cancer. Never mind my head, being around you makes my asshole hurt. God is punishing me for some reason by having you in my class. I don't have to teach you to be a waste of life, you already are." Every second of my time in school was a living hell. When I was four years old I couldn't wait to start school the next year because I thought it'd be fun. I can't think of anything more opposite of fun. A lot of people fucked with me too, not just that filthy lowlife slut.

My life just got more and more fucked as I went through High School. The kids in gym felt that breaking a mirror brought more luck than picking me for teams, girls laughed at me, I had absolutely no friends to speak of and *teachers would fail me on purpose for spite. They would return the essays I wrote with F's and comments like, "You clearly weren't paying attention in class, Ronnie, because you're offering your opinion when I already told you what your thoughts should be on this."*

Sometimes, those so-called "teachers" would read my work out loud to the class and encourage them to mock me, hit me and hate me for having my own thoughts on subjects.

I wanted all my teachers dead or fired. Most days I ignored their bullshit but when I couldn't, I'd get into these heated arguments with them. It was always about how I failed to go along with "the program." They especially hated when I told them how they were fucking sheep who did whatever they were told and their hypocritical and repressive ways would mean the end of civilization. No matter how strong a point I made, I always ended up suspended. Adults in faux positions of power don't like to be told how fucking stupid they are.

I was dragged violently by my hair into Carpenter Hell Nuthouse five years ago, when I was still seventeen years old. My folks, who I hope fucking die, wanted me committed before I was officially an adult so they could ensure I'd be locked up for a long time. They too, felt I was crazy because I questioned "the system." It was barely dawn, on the coldest day in February, when my bedroom door was kicked in by these two gorilla-sized fuckers. One of them held my face down with his boot while the other one cuffed my hands and feet. They threw me into their truck, face first. I screamed and cursed at my parents through a small window for what they were doing to me. I knew those ignorant, heartless morons were praying that'd be the last they see of me. My father even flipped me off.

The whole time I've been trapped here a bunch of quacks have taken turns with me. Each brainless maggot has been more cruel than the last. There was this one who I knew had a rep for forcing patients to blow him. He tried that shit with me and I bit one of his balls clean off. That was a good time. The attendants here are just as bad. Worse. Where the fuck do they find these depraved creatures? Sick, sadistic fucks, every last one of them.

Never forget when you're in a shit-hole like Carpenter Hell that no one wants you to get better. No one wants you to get out. All they want is to see you suffer and then die from the insanity <u>they</u> caused. The insanity <u>they</u> labeled you with. They will never let up until they finally break you. Once, during a group session I refused to take part in the discussion so the doctor said if I didn't want to draw attention to myself by interacting with everyone then he would create attention for me. That motherfucker got two of those beastly attendants to rip my clothes off and I had to sit there for the next hour, completely naked in full view of everyone. Then he let the group take turns smacking me and spitting in my face. I thought of that rotten cunt, Ms. Lawler. Carpenter Hell is what made me this insane man. This broken man.

There isn't a single person here who is interested in helping anyone. They constantly remind you how unimportant you are. They tell you that they could kill you and no one would give a shit. They tell you that as long as they are there, you will never see anything beyond the walls of Carpenter Hell. They won't let you infect society with your crazy, free-thinking ways. I pray that they kill me. I am so miserable. I might have been considered an intelligent, individualistic man in some parts of the world if I wasn't forced into this goddamn place. There is no hope here. There is only the guarantee that life will always be shit.

Fuck, they're coming to get me. I'm scheduled for experimental treatment again. They'll torture me until I admit insanity then they'll heavily drug me and stick me in front of a T.V. with a bunch of other drooling maniacs. Last time they put on Bloodsucking Freaks.

Don't forget my words. There is NO hope at Carpenter Hell. Don't give in. Let them try to destroy your mind and your will to live but take comfort in the fact that you're not crazy. THEY did this TO you!

I'm not crazy,

Ronnie

JUNE 28TH

Dear Patricia,

I miss you so much, sweetheart. You have no idea. Every day that I haven't gotten to see my little girl growing up has been torture. It still hurts at this very second and will continue to eat me up as each day passes that I'm not a part of your life. I just wish you would give me another chance.

I know your mother has probably told you a ton of horrible things about me. That's not to say she is completely to blame for our relationship--or lack thereof. There are a million things I wish I could take back but I can't. All I could do is apologize for my mistakes and do my best to not repeat them.

I'm not sure what you've heard so I'll just tell you some stuff I'm guilty of without fabrication and it'll be up to you to decide whether that changes anything between us. Okay, princess?

First off, it's true that I was an alcoholic for a number of years. I had a problem. I would get down about stuff and I relied on booze to deal with those issues. It wasn't the smart thing to do, that's for sure, but when people are sad we all deal with it differently. My way just happened to be one of the worst ways to solve any dilemma.

Your mom tried to help me. I will never dispute that. Some people might have run away as fast as they could the second they realized they married the town drunk but she never considered that as an option early on. Sometimes she tried being extra loving with me, thinking perhaps if I was happy all the time there'd be no reason to drink so much. This worked once in a while and you could just tell it took so much out of her. Not that being extra affectionate was hard for her--your mother's heart is almost too big for her little body.

It's nerve wrecking though, when you put so much effort into doing something nice for someone and it could all backfire in a second--especially when that someone is really drunk and capable of drastically switching moods without any notice. I give your mom a lot of credit. She probably says lots of things about me that aren't true or exaggerated but I'd never deny the hell I put her through.

We were happy for a while though. It wasn't all bad. I met your mother, believe it or not, in church. I was a very different person back then. I had so much faith. The world was my oyster. In fact, I blame your mother for my loss of interest in religion. She was so pretty, how could I possibly concentrate on what was being said at mass? After two months of ignoring God's word, I got up the courage to ask her out.

THE FUNERAL PORTRAIT

Our first date was the Florida State Fair. We stuffed our faces with hot dogs, roasted corn on the cobb, popcorn and cotton candy. Really, I was the one stuffing my face since I didn't get a chance to eat dinner that night. Your mom just snacked here and there. She was so lady-like the whole night, even being so kind to not point out the big mustard stain I had on my shirt from the stupid hotdogs.

I knew I loved her then or at least I knew that I would love her. A year later we were married and I was the happiest I had ever been. My drinking was under control and it was only a social thing, nothing more. We tried having children right away but with no luck. I had my job at the post office and your mom had that job at the attorney's office. Things were good.

A couple of years went by and I was slowly becoming more difficult to live with. I got passed up for a promotion at work and hit the bottle pretty hard. I guess your mother thought it would be a one-time thing, but I began dealing with all of our problems like that. We couldn't even make love, because I was too drunk most nights.

Our marriage wasn't going that great so unlike me, who thought liquor was the best solution, your mom thought having the child we always wanted would turn things around. I didn't know she was taking fertility pills at the time. There was a lot I didn't know. Mostly because I wasn't sober enough to notice anyway.

Somehow, we managed to conceive. Not to be graphic or anything, sweetheart, but the way I was most nights, it's a miracle your mother got me to knock her up. I didn't remember it at all. I know it's really horrible for me to tell you that I have no recollection of the moment your mom and I created you, but I'm trying to be honest. I don't want to keep anything from you, Patty. I want you to trust me.

A short time later you were born and I'll tell you, even the cutest babies look like little trolls when they're first born but you were beautiful the moment you came out. No kidding. Everyone at the hospital fell in love with you right away. I couldn't believe I was half responsible for another living human being--especially such an adorable one.

I promised your mother that I wouldn't drink when you were born, not even to celebrate. I stuck by my promise for a few months but I fell off the wagon and it wasn't pretty. They say postpartum depression usually only affects women but it seemed as though it skipped your mom over and took up residence in me.

Don't be misled, I did love you. I adored you so very, very much but I wasn't your mom's favorite anymore. Anyone who knew us would say I wasn't her favorite way before you came along and I'd say that they've got a great argument.

Even when your mother trusted me enough to hold you, I refused. I wouldn't have hurt you, sweetheart. I can't explain it. It's like being demoted and then your boss wants you to train the person who is taking your position. Ya know? So the idea of having a baby to bring us closer together pulled us apart even more.

My drinking got worse and I developed a cocaine habit on top of that. I was able to keep that from your mom for the first couple of years of your life. I did it infrequently enough to go unnoticed. By the time you were three though there was no denying it. I was squandering our money and looked like hell. I'm not sure if your mother still loved me then but perhaps for your sake, she gave me one more chance to get clean.

I didn't think rehab was what I needed and that I could kick my bad habits on my own. That was a huge mistake. I should have known that at the time but I wasn't in the best frame of mind. It came to a head when I didn't come home one night. Your mom left you with one of our neighbors and went looking for me.

When she found me I had already blown my entire paycheck on drugs and alcohol. I was unconscious on a park bench and to make matters worse I had urinated on myself. If I were on the opposite spectrum of this ordeal, I would have left me there on that bench to rot and hope that my kid never has to see what a pathetic loser their father is. Not your mother though. She pretty much physically dragged me to her car and tossed me in.

She had already arranged for you to spend the night with the neighbor that had been watching you because she planned to have it out with me. We argued for hours. I can't possibly imagine what I might have been saying in my defense because the way I look at it now--there was no excuse for my behavior. I can't rationalize anything I did back then and I've paid the price every day since.

Your mom, God bless her, was great at arguing. I think it was from being around all those lawyers at work. It didn't matter if I wasn't wasted, I couldn't talk my way out of anything once she got going. I knew that. She knew that. That's probably why she kept going even though I told her to stop. She kept twisting that knife deeper and deeper into me until I snapped.

I shouldn't have hit her. That's an even worse way to deal with anger or depression than all the toxins I was ingesting. Don't you ever let your significant other hit you, baby. If they dare to pull that whole "I hit you out of love" bullshit you let me know and I swear to God I will kill them immediately. I won't think twice about it. If you love someone, you don't do that to them. There's no debate.

When I hit your mother, all the anger I felt left me. The effects of my drug and alcohol binge disappeared in a flash. It was all replaced with a four ton dose of regret that was so heavy it literally brought me to my knees. I was so used to your mom being angry at me all the time that when I hit her, I was surprised that it wasn't anger I saw in her face. It was hurt. Not just physical hurt. Internal pain and suffering.

She looked to me, lips trembling as she cried and without actually speaking a single word I could hear her voice in my head saying, "What happened to us? When did everything go so wrong?" I had put our whole life into perspective with one punch. That's how many times I hit your mom. Once. And once was too much.

I should've put my arms around her and begged her forgiveness. I should've kissed her and told her how lucky I was to have her. There're a lot of things I should've done right there. In actuality what I ended up doing was kneeling there, quietly, as your mother packed up some of her belongings as well as yours. She didn't say anything before she left but I did hear her stop at the front door and cry some more. This really broke my heart. That part of our lives was over.

Through her connections at work she was able to finalize her divorce from me in record time. When it came to custody of you, I didn't put up any sort of fight. How could I possibly care for a child in my condition? No judge, in their right mind, would subject a minor to my lifestyle. It was amazing that I had never been arrested, now that I think about it.

I lost your mother. I lost you. So in a sense, I lost myself. You both moved away to Georgia and I made no effort to stay in touch. The door was open initially and I let it close. I know that. I am truly sorry.

After you were both gone I thought about killing myself several times. Your dad only seeks out crappy ways to resolve things it seems. Now I'm going to pull the whole "do as I say, not as I do" card here because suicide should never be an option but for me, it was the only sensible answer. Without you, I had nothing to live for. I'm not saying that to make you feel guilty by any means. I wasn't there for you and you have every right to not want me in your life. I'm just hoping, praying, that you will consider giving your old man another chance.

Your mother would never take me back in a thousand lifetimes, even though I've conquered my addictions. I'd think she was crazy if she did, but there's still hope for you and me to be friends. I don't expect you to give me

213

any type of fatherly respect, but I'd love to start out by being your friend at least.

Without you in my life, sweetheart, I still have nothing to live for. And again, I'm not saying that to make you feel bad or anything, it's just to illustrate how much you mean to me. That I'd rather be dead than go on knowing my little girl doesn't want to know her daddy.

It's been ten years since I last saw you. Aside from my eyes, you looked just like your mother so you must be prettier than ever. You're also old enough now to make your own decisions about certain things. I think this is one of them. We don't have to be strangers if you don't want to be.

I love you so much, Patricia. I beg you to please give me a chance to be in your life again. I was a fool and I did my time. Please let me leave this cage and see my little girl. I can't do a life sentence, sweetheart. It hurts too much.

We can take it really slow. Just write back if you're interested. Anything from you would be great. I'd be the happiest man alive to even get just a postcard from you that said "hi." I can't tell you enough how much I love you. I hope my princess will find it in her heart to forgive the stupid man I used to be and allow the better man I am now to be there for her.

Your Loving Dad,

Joseph Kovac
P.S. Wish your mother well for me.

APRIL 25TH

Dear Diary,

Yet another stressful day in the life of Constance Bergman. I'm starting to wonder why I even bother. It doesn't help that I work as a server and have to fake being all smiley and happy with people every day. I've never been a depressed person before so I don't understand why all of a sudden things are affecting me. I probably caught it from Guy. That is one unhappy dude. Can't say I'm not partly responsible for that but he was always kind of a downer so it's not all on me.

He came to see me again the other day. It's like being stalked but not in a threatening way, just annoying. I never understood what his problem was but I think I'm beginning to make sense of it. We were only together for five months really. He said he loved me and I believed him but I wasn't looking for love at the time. Not to sound like a slut or anything but I just wanted a steady dick. I could get some whenever I wanted but it made me feel like a skank to only make booty calls. It's nice when you have that one person there to satisfy you when you need it. I guess Guy interpreted that as "Until Death Do Us Part" but it was simple monogamy.

All for nothing since I ended up cheating on him anyways. I never told him that though and I never will. I can be a bitch sometimes, but that would kill him. Literary, kill him. That was over two years ago and I know that doesn't seem too deep in the past but I've matured a lot since then.

Guy always treated me like a princess. He really was wonderful but like I said, I didn't want to get swept off my feet. I just wanted fun. It was one of those days when he was really annoying the piss out of me with his I love you this and I love you that. So I made up some story about staying in because I was sick. That almost backfired because he insisted on coming over to take care of me. After like an hour of convincing him that all I needed was sleep and that I'd call him the next day he finally let it go.

I ended up going over to a friend's house to hangout. He shall remain nameless. We smoked some pot and got pretty drunk. I remember dozing off on his bed for a few and when I woke up my friend was slobbering all over my tits and his hand was down my pants. I kind of pushed him away at first but then I thought of Guy and how he was probably going to be up all night worrying about me and it seemed pathetic. I started giggling at the thought. I was so wasted at that point too that I just closed my eyes and drifted off to unconsciousness, content to let my friend do whatever he wanted to me after I passed out. And do a lot he certainly did. How do I know? The bastard videotaped the whole thing.

For the next couple of weeks he used that videotape to constantly blackmail me into sex. I was his personal, and free, prostitute. I never felt so gross and used in all of my life. You know why I did it though? Because of Guy. I didn't want him to find out about the tape. I didn't want to hurt him like that but there was only so much I could put up with. So rather than have Guy find out what was going on and be crushed, I dumped him. I wasn't lying though when I told him I wasn't interested in something long term or that I didn't love him. In some ways, that tape just sped up the process of what was already unavoidable.

During my final visit to my friend's house, he fell asleep after I rocked his world. Hey, I didn't really wanna fuck him, but I wasn't gonna just lie there like a dead fish and have word get around that I'm a lousy lay.

I was able to steal the tape from him while he was napping. That idiot never thought to make a backup copy. Even I would have done that. I'm glad he didn't though because I wasn't ready to be the latest internet porn sensation.

I don't know why I've never written this down before. I've just been thinking about my own life and the decisions I've made after breaking up with (what has turned out to be) the nicest guy I've ever dated. He's been this sad, pathetic, loser in my book for so long that I didn't notice I was the sad, pathetic, loser all along. It just took me some time to find that out. I pushed someone away because they loved me and wanted to make me happy. How fucking stupid does that sound?

I could never be with Guy, that's for sure. We'd drive each other crazy. Well...he'd drive me crazy. He is super sweet. Insanely considerate and

217

surprisingly very adequate in the bedroom but he doesn't seem to take charge of anything. He doesn't put up a fight. When I broke up with him he asked me why I was doing it. I made up some bullshit on the spot and he just put his head down, muttered, "Okay" and let me walk away. He can love you like you wouldn't believe but he hates himself. If you want to share your life with other people the way he envisions, you should at least like yourself and I don't think he even can say that about himself.

Part of me wants to call him up and tell him all of this. Tell him that I'm sorry about how cold I was (am.) Tell him that I love him in retrospect. Tell him that every man I've been with since him has treated me like a worthless whore. Tell him that most nights I cry myself to sleep thinking about what a ruin my life has become. Let him know how every time I see him it reminds me of how stupid I am and I get so angry that I take it out on him. Maybe I would even tell Guy about the time, when I was dating this asshole cop, that I put his gun in my mouth one night while he slept. With my finger on the trigger, I cried and I cried and I wondered if this was how Guy felt when I broke his heart.

I can't tell you how much I would love to be with Guy. It wouldn't work right now though. Maybe some time down the line if things changed. I have a lot of shit to clear out of my head. He also has some changes to make in order for us to happily co-exist. It would be nice but I couldn't tell him how I feel. We're still not ready for each other and if we rushed back into something before then, we could ruin it forever.

I definitely have to make a conscience effort to be nicer to him when he comes around too. If he even comes around again after the way I've been. I've got to stop letting whatever douche I'm sleeping with that month make me a bitch with everyone.

Guy. Guy Edwards. Constance. Constance Bergman. Constance Edwards. Guy and Constance sitting in a tree...K-I-S-S-I...

I want to kiss him,

Constance

MAY 31ST

From the desk of Dr. Anthony Petersen:

Have I really helped anyone? Up here on my high horse looking down my nose at people I am ashamed to call what I do therapy. Aromatherapy is more useful than I am. Guy pointed that out quite clearly. All these years it seems I was just getting people to ignore their problems instead of dealing with them. I was paying more attention to the clock when I should have been paying attention to what was really wrong with my patients. Everyone is different and I treated them all the same. Making them feel guilty for their imperfections as if I was without a single screw out of place. Who the hell do I think I am?

Can you believe how much I've let a patient get to me? I can't believe it myself but it's true and I know I have to change my approach in some way or I will never feel like I did any good with the knowledge I spent so many years in school to obtain. Maybe down the line people will leave my office actually cured of whatever it is that ails them, but right now I'd have to agree with Guy. I am a failure. At least that's how I feel as a doctor.

THE FUNERAL PORTRAIT

My dear, sweet, Anne, please tell me I'm not a failure at being a husband. Please tell me I've made a happy home for us. Please tell me I haven't failed you.

Your loving husband,

Anthony Petersen

JUNE 11TH

To Whom It Concern:

Let it be known that I don't give a fuck about anything. Anything. No exceptions. No one has ever cared whether I'm alive or dead so why should I give a shit about anyone else? And I know what you're gonna say--that's just bitterness talking, Gus. You've gotta look beyond all that bullshit and live your life for yourself. Don't worry about what people have done to you in the past.

That's exactly what I'm doing--living life for myself. When my father walked out on us, even though I was only six, I didn't cry about it. Then when my mother remarried a couple of years later and my step-dad would kick the shit out me with his steel toe boots, I took it like a man. When I caught him nailing my thirteen year old sister and he told us not to tell our mom or he'd kill all three of us, I barely flinched. When he died in a car crash along with my sister and mom a year later, no one could accuse me of shedding tears because I never did.

THE FUNERAL PORTRAIT

I was glad they were dead. My sister would have grown up to be the deranged, local whore anyway after being forced to suck and fuck my step-dad all the time. He deserved to die for so many reasons. I wish I could have killed him myself. And my mom deserved to die for being stupid and desperate enough to marry a fucking scumbag like that. I don't know if she was in denial or if she really was that brainless to not notice what was going on between her daughter and husband. I would've figured it out, even if I hadn't seen him in the act.

I was standing by the bedroom, looking in through a small opening in the door. My sister knew I was standing there because she just stared at the door, crying and wincing in pain as quietly as possible. It was mostly drowned out by the sound of the bed squeaking where he had her bent over, the loud clapping each time their bodies smacked together and his horrible grunting, especially when he finished up.

I was so lost in my sympathy for my sister and blind rage that I couldn't scramble away fast enough when he suddenly pulled open the door. My step-dad grabbed me by the hair and flung me on the bed with my half-naked sister. She was lying on her side, facing away from me. I didn't mean to look but I could see she had blood running down the inside of her thighs all the way to her calves. That's when he threatened to kill us and our mom if we said anything. I didn't care if he killed me, but I knew my sister was scared so I agreed to keep quiet for her sake.

If they hadn't died in that car accident I probably would have killed all three of them myself soon enough. I've always preferred to handle my own

223

situations. Leave as little to chance as possible, I say. Everyone is always begging for help and praying to God for this and that. I say fuck those people! Maybe if they spent less time crying and complaining about the bad hand they've been dealt they could actually do something with their lives. But they don't because, ultimately, their lives are shit anyway.

So blame it on God that you're so fucking dumb. He insisted that you spend the afternoon with Him, destroying mailboxes instead of doing your homework. Blame it on God that you put on two hundred pounds. He's the one that gave you that fridge that immaculately conceives tubs of ice cream and microwave fried chicken on a daily basis. Blame God for your rotten teeth. He created the Heavens and Earth in six days but never found time during that seventh day of rest to create toothpaste. How could anyone be so thoughtless?

I'm not a religious man so I can't tell you how much I hate when people put every aspect of their lives in God's hands. Maybe He wants you to do some shit for yourself. He's not going to wash your fucking car and he most certainly isn't going to remind you to pay your credit card bills on time. It's not fate that you're watching the same stupid ass infomercial over and over where they're selling those blankets you wear which are essentially just backwards robes so you have to buy one--you're just too goddamn lazy to get up and change the channel. Like everything in your life, you're incapable of standing up and making something happen on your own.

I have to admit though, the more I think about it, maybe God is to blame for all of your troubles because if I were God I would do all of these bad things to you and you would deserve it. Lucky for you I'm not but you can still pray to me. My name also starts with a "G" and is just as short. Chances are, me not being God and all, I won't hear your prayer. I encourage you to keep trying though. Maybe someday, through some crazy telepathic wormhole in our universe I will receive your message for help. And if you do somehow manage to get through to me while praying, don't expect me to give a fuck.

Sincerely Insincere,

Gus

EVEN IN THE SUN THE DARKNESS FINDS ME

JULY 3RD

Dear Mom and Dad,

I have been giving my current status a lot of thought the past week. The way things have played out with Tallulah makes one undeniable fact keep coming back to me no matter how many different angles I look at our relationship from.

I love her. Plain and simple--I love her.

I'm so scared though because I think she possibly loves me too but I don't know how to bring it up. The last person I loved didn't love me back and you all know how that turned out. I don't think Tallulah would be rude about it the way Constance was, but what if she doesn't want to be loved? It is possible. I mean, why would she have me trying to kill her if she was interested in making a happy life with me? Right? Maybe I'm enjoying this criss-cross, murder/suicide thing too much. Not the killing part of it. I'd be scared of myself if I got desensitized to that. It still freaks me out, I'm just better at hiding it now.

It's the spending time with Tallulah part I love. I love that she looks forward to the new ways I think up to help her die. I love how emotional she gets when I really put forth an effort and kill her in a romantic way. I love how sometimes she says things like, "Why don't we blow off dying today and get some tacos?" I love how much she believes I am capable of the task at hand. I love how whenever one of my ideas doesn't work out she kisses me and says, "Don't worry, big boy. We'll get'em next time." I love how much she depends on me to put an end to her suffering. I love how alive she is on the outside, even if she's been dead inside for years. I love how alive she makes me feel when I'm around her.

I love everything about this woman and I'm scared out of my fucking mind that I'm going to lose it all. If she does in fact love me, I can try to convince her to stick around but she could be so far along in her sadness that my love won't be enough. Doesn't it make sense though that if your whole life was shit, you'd hold on to anything that made you forget about your past troubles? I would. I don't need to kill myself, I just wanted to. With someone like Tallulah around though, why the fuck would I? I could be happy. Happy people don't commit suicide.

I have to tell her. I will probably ruin everything but I have to tell her. For all I know this could be what she really needs, not death. Maybe she will fall into my arms and thank me for loving her more than anyone ever has, because I do. Maybe she'll smile and say, "So that's why you haven't been trying to kill me lately? I love you too, Guy. I don't want to die. I want to live so that we can be in love forever."

Forever isn't that long for those of us who are mortal but I will love her with every breath I have left in life. She has shown me that no matter how bleak things can get, as long as you're alive there is always hope. Things could get worse, you never know, but sometimes they go the other way. Sometimes the sun shines on your side of the street so you've got to hold on. I've never thought that way. She did that. The most unhappy person in the whole wide world, taught me to be optimistic. I would've never believed that to be possible before she insisted I light her cigarette on the roof that day. I need to take a chance. I only hope her heart hasn't closed up shop for good. We'll see.

By the way and before I forget, I just wanted to let you in on more of your lovely son's tomfoolery. I'm talking about Bruno of course. Aside from trying to kill my girlfriend just about every other day, I don't do much that would be considered uncouth. Bruno, however...well, let's just say he's the kind of guy television networks created the three-second delay for during live broadcasts so they have time to edit out any inappropriate behavior.

I went by the pet store to bring him a bag of funnel cakes he had forgotten on the kitchen table. He demanded that I bring them to him at work and even offered to pay for my gas if I did. (He didn't.) So I brought him his bag of funnel cakes but as I approached the aisle he was in, I overheard him dealing with a customer and hung back until he was done. It was an old woman looking to buy a scratching post for her cat. This is more or less how your wonderful son dealt with this lady, who could very well be someone's grandmother.

"Excuse me, young man?"

Yeah, what do you want?

"Do you have any scratching posts for cats?"

Yeah, there's a bunch right behind you.

"Oh, no, I saw those."

Oh, good. Well, then turn around and you'll see them again. I promise.

"Young man?"

What?!

"Those scratching posts are not going to do?"

What's wrong with them?

"My little Rosie doesn't know her own strength and she'd tear those to pieces in a week. She's too frisky for her own good."

How long do you expect a scratching post to last?

"Well, at least a month."

So buy four.

"You are so silly. Where would I possibly put four scratching posts?"

I could tell you some place I'd like to put a scratching post right now.

"I just need something strong and sturdy that will satisfy my Rosie."

You know I think we have something even better than a scratching post.

"Oh. Really? What's that?

We've got this one cat in the back who's the horniest thing that's ever lived. You should see the little fucker. Yesterday, I gave him a filet of fish and he humped the hell out of that thing before he finally ate it. I think Rosie

229

would like that much better than some stupid, boring scratching post. Don't you?

"Young man, that is a terrible thing to say."

What if I said this instead? Nothing would please me more than to stretch the skin from your neck over your face to the back of your head, staple it there and then smack you around with a bat like a shit-filled piñata?

That poor old woman looked absolutely mortified. She couldn't even find the words to respond. I wouldn't be surprised if she got back in her car and just dropped dead behind the wheel out of shock. I do think if there's anyone on this Earth who could offend someone to death, it's Bruno. He even had the nerve to say "Come back soon" as the frightened old lady scrambled for the exit.

Always a man of the people.

Then Bruno sees me with the bag of funnel cakes and snatches it from my hand. He wanted to know if I took any of them and when I said I hadn't, he insisted on smelling my breath. "If you did have any of my funnel cakes, the big pile of shit you obviously ate afterwards covered the scent." Lord, give me patience.

He ordered me to tell him what I was doing with the rest of my day. I told Bruno I had to do something and it didn't concern him. That got me grabbed and slammed up against one of the shelves. A bag of cat litter busted open behind me and poured over the both of us. Me, mostly. "You better not be going to see that bitch, Constance, again. I'll dunk your head in the big fish tank again. I swear to God!" I wasn't, I just wanted to get the hell out of there.

THE FUNERAL PORTRAIT

I hate the smell of pet stores. That's probably why I hate being home so much. Practically that whole bag of litter had rained down on me by the time I was able to convince him Constance didn't play a factor in my plans for that afternoon or evening. I think it was the clumping kind.

Well, I'm off to talk to Tallulah and tell her how I feel. I'm so nervous. But like I said, I have to take a chance. The worst that could happen is either she isn't in love with me or my love isn't enough for her. That's it.

Yeah, I'd rather get hit by a bus that's engulfed in flames. That would be more pleasing than any of the above outcomes.

Wish me luck,
Guy

ACCEPTING DENIAL

JULY 4TH

To My Dear Family,

Oh, God! Oh, God I want to die! I want to fucking die right this fucking second! I can barely see what I'm writing, I'm crying so much. I can't do this. This hurts so goddamn much. I have to. I have to do it. Mom, I love you. Dad, I love you too. Bruno, I'm sorry I was never a better friend and brother but I love you as well. I can't. I can't. I can't.

She...Tallulah, won't let me save her with love. She'd rather be dead than take a chance on my love. Can you believe that? Does that make any fucking sense, whatsoever? I don't wanna live. I do not want to live!

...

Okay, I've calmed down a bit. I'm just so hurt. It's not like I'm a stranger to rejection, it's just I truly do not understand why I'm being shot down this time. Every girl I've ever been with has eventually dumped me. I've never broken up with anyone. And to be honest, I've understood each time why they didn't want to be with me. I didn't see the reasoning behind Constance's behavior before, but I do now. I still think she is a manipulative little bitch but I probably smothered her. She was just looking to have a good time and I was thinking marriage and kids. I've always been like that from my very first girlfriend.

Gaylen Cardille. She was as hot as they came in High School. We hooked up during our freshman year. After an hour of making out I start talking about how much I want to get married and buy a nice two-story house to fill with children and all this stupid shit no other guy at school, who wasn't a complete fucking loser idiot, would bring up right after a sexy girl takes off her top and says she wants you to be her first.

I remember the look on her face. It was pity. She actually felt sorry for me because she knew I'd struggle with women for the rest of my life. And she was right. Gaylen sat there on my bed, with her amazing breasts exposed for my taking and said, in a very disappointed tone, "I'm sorry. I think I gave you the wrong idea. I was just looking to pop my cherry; maybe even see what giving a blowjob is like and you seemed like a nice enough guy to do it with. I should go." In a matter of seconds she was dressed and gone. I would even find out later that while walking home from our house, one of the seniors from the football team spotted her and struck up a conversation. That very same night he made sure she had tons of different firsts in the bedroom.

She didn't give me the wrong idea. I gave me the wrong idea. I always do. I'm my own cock blocker. And I want to tell you what happened tonight but I don't want to have to think of the words to describe it, so I'm just going to write what was said, exactly.

We were sitting in the living room watching a movie. I had barely said a word all night. I know it's not unusual to be quiet while watching a movie but even before it started, I wasn't really talking. I wasn't reacting to what we were watching either. She noticed.

"You're so quiet tonight, Guy."

Really? I hadn't noticed. I, uh...I guess I was just thinking.

"Oh. Were you thinking about why you haven't tried to kill me for almost two weeks now?"

Huh?

"You heard me."

I don't know.

"What's that supposed to mean?"

I just...forgot. That's all.

"You forgot? And what have we been doing this whole time--playing house?"

I'm sorry. I didn't think about it. I guess I've been having too much...fun.

"Oh, that's the reason. You've been having fun. I see now."

…

"You think this is fun?"

…

"This is not fun, Guy. This is my life."

I know it's your life. I know all about your life.

"Yeah, you do. I've told you everything about me; every little detail. So what I can't understand is how you can fucking sit there and think, for a second, of this as fun."

I know your life hasn't been fun. That's not I was talking about.

"Then what are you talking about? Fill me in, so that I can better understand you."

You! I've been having fun with you!

"Don't do that."

Don't do what?

"You know what you're doing."

I'm sorry. I've just really been enjoying your company.

"Stop it!" (Tallulah smashed a vase of flowers against the wall.) "We had a deal! Remember?!"

Yes, I do, but I just...Tallulah, I...

"Don't you dare. Don't you fucking dare!"

Tallulah, I love you.

"No! No! You can't!"

I do.

"No!"

Why not?

"You know what I've been through and you know what I have to do."

But why? (I took a step towards her and she took a step back)

"Don't come near me. I mean it."

Why do you have to kill yourself?

"Because I can't take this fucking life anymore! I need to do this."

I don't understand that. Don't you enjoy your time with me?

"Of course I do."

Then what's the problem?! I'm fucked in the head and you're fucked in the head, but when we're together none of that shit matters. Together we can be happy like normal people. Can't you see that?

"Guy, I...I was afraid this would happen." (Tallulah walked over to me, standing just a foot away.) "Please don't think I don't love you. I do. I love you more than I thought possible with what's left of my heart. But I have gone through too much shit in my life and I simply cannot do this anymore. What I show to you isn't all there is to me. You mostly get the good stuff. The carefree, laughing Tallulah you love being around comes out when you're around. But when you're not there, the real me takes over and it's an endless fucking nightmare of screaming and crying. Slashing my wrists and cutting my throat over and over again, begging God to give up on me. If you saw all of that you would know what the truth is. And the truth is it's too late to save me. I don't want to hurt you like this but even your love, as wonderful as it is, can't save me now." (All I could do was stand there, staring at her through my tear-soaked eyes) "I'm sorry. Death is the only solution for me."

Well, your solution sucks.

I walked out of her house, slamming the front door behind me. As I stood on the front porch I could hear her crying inside. It was a painful, gut wrenching, uncontrollable type of crying that brought violent dry heaves. More glass was shattering too. I don't care. She doesn't want me. What the fuck have I got to be optimistic about anymore? Let her find someone else to figure out why she can't die. I'm done.

THE FUNERAL PORTRAIT

After you read this, have the police go to the glass factory. They will find my body in the back parking lot. I don't want any of you accompanying them there. I don't want you to see me like that. I'm sure Bates will give you a good rate on my funeral. I'd like to think he'd do it for free but that bastard wouldn't bury one of his own relatives unless they left a deposit.

Forget about open casket as well. I will be too messed up from the fall and I don't trust Devlin to make me presentable enough for viewing. I don't want any fanfare, just toss me in whatever coffin, say your goodbyes and stick me in the ground. All I ask is if you get me a tombstone, for it to say...

...

...I can't even think of something worth writing. Pathetic. Don't put anything at all. The less people know about me the better. I'd hate to think that hundreds of years from now some archaeologist might unearth my grave site and put forth tremendous efforts to discover who I was and what my life was like. Quite like my life, it'd be a complete waste of time.

I love you,

Guy Edwards

JULY 8TH

To My Dear Family,

My last letter really felt like the one. I honestly believed I'd be dead by now. My problem (amongst the many) is that I think too much. So much in fact that I couldn't do what I set out to do when I went to the glass factory. I kept going over everything in my head to the point I had a migraine and just wanted to lay down.

However, I ended up having a revelation yesterday. It came to me in the form of more sadness. In all of my misery I lost sight of certain things and one of them caught me off guard. Some things are inevitable but you can't help but react a certain way, regardless of how much you try. Today, I'm very down but in a different way. This doesn't have to do with me. I've been so selfish with my suffering. I sometimes forget that other people suffer too. Other people lose what's important to them. Today is for them.

Initially, I had asked Bates for a couple of days off to stew but I felt like going in on the second day. I had to do something to keep my mind occupied with other stuff. Work was always great for distracting me from any problems I've had because when I'm working that's all I focus on. I can't afford to ruin someone's last memory of a loved one because I fell asleep behind the wheel. (Minus that one guy I over-filled with embalming fluid.)

238

I should have known something was up because as soon as I walked in, Bates looked really surprised to see me. Not surprised so much as alarmed. He scurried over and blocked my path to the embalming room. "Guy, you're not supposed to be in today." I knew that but I didn't feel like being home anymore. I was restless.

I tried walking past him and he moved with me so I couldn't get by. I was in no mood for this and I've never really spoken back to Bates before but I told him that I was having a terrible week and really couldn't take much more shit from anyone. "I wasn't going to give you shit, Guy. I just wanted to, uh..." How frustrating it was to watch him not find the words. What? You just wanted to what?!

"It's just that there's a body back there." Yeah. So what? There's a body back there almost every day. That's part of life, isn't it? Dying? "Yeah, but you know this person." Judging by Bates' reaction, I probably lost all of the color in my face just then. I tried to speak but barely got out a whisper. Who?

It was Mr. Friar. No! No! No!

I'm not an idiot. I knew his days were numbered. He was old but he's one of those people that you enjoy having around so much you can't picture him eventually not being there, despite the obvious. I know it's crazy but part of me felt like it was my fault. I'd been neglecting my friend. I hadn't been by his peach stand for at least a month or so. Maybe no one had. Maybe he died of loneliness, like Mr. Sebastian Alexander.

The thought of Friar lying in his small room at the retirement community, thinking he finally had no one. There was his son in Georgia, who wasn't a bad guy or anything but didn't have time to visit much and there was me, his best customer. He probably thought my absence was caused by me doing something foolish, like jumping off of a factory rooftop. Friar wouldn't approve of such actions and I'd be so embarrassed to think wherever he is now that he could see me doing that.

The only thing that kept me from really letting the tears come forth was the awkwardness of Bates' handling of the situation. I've seen him deal with grieving people day in and day out with the same cold confidence he's had since I've met him but he looked like a beginner now in front of me. There was something comical about it.

"I'm sorry, Guy. I didn't expect you to come in. Devlin is out at the moment but he's going to take care of it. You don't even have to go back there." I told him that I could do it. I've looked death in the face more times than I cared to remember. What's once more?

"No, no, no. We're not embalming or holding a service for him here. The old man is getting cremated. His son is coming in today to settle the paperwork and pick up the remains. Devlin and I have it all under control." I wanted to at least say goodbye to my friend before he went into the retort. That's what you call the chamber where the body is placed in the cremator. I always found this to be ironic since most people would say a retort is a quick and clever comeback but when you go into our retort, you sure as hell won't be coming back.

I guess some small parts of you are. Bone fragments anyway. That's a common misconception with a lot of people when it comes to cremations. Many people think its actual ash we put into urns. Really, it's those bone fragments left over from the cremation. We put them in this machine called a cremulator which pulverizes the fragments into that light gray sand everyone assumes is just ashes.

Some cremulators can still leave behind little chips, noticeable upon closer inspection but we have a really good one. It grinds everything down perfectly. But like I already told you, cremations are the only thing Bates will not take part in at all. He must've been really worried about me to be helping Devlin with this one, even though I'm sure his end would probably only consist of the paperwork.

"Okay, you can go say bye to the old guy but then I want you to let me and Devlin deal with this. And if you...you know, wanna talk or something...I'm not very good with this sort of thing when it really counts, but whatever you need, you just let me know." I felt bad for writing such horrible things about Bates before. Having worked for him for several years and knowing what a colossal meathead he could be, I was touched by his concern.

Friar was laid out on the embalming table the way bodies usually were. Soon, Devlin and Bates would be placing him in one of our cardboard containers for cremation. No sense in throwing money away on a coffin that's going to be burned up anyway. We did have a loner though for people who got cremated but had a viewing first. Sounds creepy and gross but we always replace the lining and everything inside after each use so it's not a big deal.

It's funny how when you view the body of an elderly person they just look like they're sleeping. When they're still alive though and are actually sleeping, they often look dead. Friar looked like he was sleeping. Just taking a nap. If he could, he'd say, "It's almost noon and I saw this table here so I figured, what the hell. It's nap time."

I can't believe how much I ignored him towards the end. He was the one person who always gave me such great advice and knew what a sorry sack of shit I was but never pointed a finger at me; never made me feel worse than I already did. Not on purpose, anyway. I wish I could talk to him now. All I can do is cry.

What's with the tears?

I'm so not ready for this.

It's all right, my boy. It's all a part of life.

I know, but I just recently got reminded how much I fucking hate that part.

Hey, there're plenty of things to hate about life but death's not worth your energy. Why bother if there's nothing you can do about it? You know there are people who spend so much time worrying about death that they actually forget to live. Isn't that something?

I understand. I just wish you weren't dead, Mr. Friar. I don't think I ever told you this but you really were my only friend.

I really appreciate you saying that, Guy, but it can't be true. There has to be someone else.

There was someone else. A woman I never got around to telling you about.

What about her?

Her? She's not my friend anymore.

Why is that?

We both want different things.

You know most people want the same thing but they don't realize there's more than one way to interpret situations.

What do you mean?

What does this friend of yours want more than anything?

Well, I guess in a nutshell, to be happy.

And what do you want?

I want her to be happy too.

So what's the problem?

We have severely different opinions on what exactly will make her happy.

Well, one of you is wrong. Really think about it, Guy. Without knowing, your way just might not be the best way to make this girl happy. Like it or not, her solution to the problem could be what she really needs and you have to be prepared to accept that. Usually the greater the sacrifice, the greater the reward.

You sure make a hell of a lot of sense, Mr. Friar. I'm really going to miss you.

I'll miss you too, Guy.

And the world just got a little emptier. Or maybe it's me I'm really talking about.

In Mourning,

Guy

VINCENT VIÑAS

JULY 10TH

To My Dear Family,

Kovac is dead. For real dead. I got a call from Gus telling me what happened. I never gave him my number. I guess Tallulah felt I should know but didn't feel the need to tell me herself. Did she want me to feel bad that Kovac was gone and I still hadn't killed her? Maybe she just figured I had spent a little time with him and it was common courtesy. I don't know. But it really angered me that it was Gus calling me and not her.

He and Kovac had just gotten some food from a drive-thru and were heading home. I didn't know Gus was staying with Kovac. The road back to their place was pitch black at night and out of the way.

There had been a car blocking their path. Its hood was up and its driver waved for them to stop. The distressed motorist was an attractive girl, probably about Gus' age. She went around to the passenger side and peered into the car. "What seems to be the trouble?" Kovac asked her. An automatic pistol was then pointed at his face from the driver's side window. "The trouble is you're still sitting in my new car," a man said.

Gus said Kovac calmly turned to look at the man with the gun and told him, "There's no fucking way you're taking this car. Not today. Not tomorrow.

245

Not ever. So fuck you and this little whore you have helping you." This pissed off the girl, who was also now pointing a gun of her own at Gus. "We should just shoot these motherfuckers and leave them on the road for the buzzards."

Kovac riled her up. "Geez, you kiss your mother/sister with that mouth?" They laughed in the car and then Gus added, "When you have a family reunion, is it just a picnic for two?" More mock laughter. Then it happened. The girl furiously demanded that Gus shut up and to ensure that he would, she smashed him in the face with the butt of her gun, accidentally discharging it. The pain and gushing blood from Gus' nose took an immediate backseat to the fact that part of Kovac's head was now missing. It was splattered in the car, on the road outside and all over the shirt of the male would-be carjacker.

Everyone froze in shock. It was the guy with the gun who first snapped out of it, opening the door and dumping Kovac onto the road. He came around the front of the car, yelling at his girl, "I can't believe you did that. Stupid bitch, you almost fucking shot me. Take the other car and get out of here!" Still in shock, she managed to scurry back to their car, slam down the hood and take off as the man pulled Gus and his bloody nose from Kovac's vehicle. He shot Gus, point-blank range three times in the chest and left him for dead as well. As he died there he could hear the Barracuda screeching away in the night.

When Gus came back to life he knew something was off. He looked over at Kovac who was lying in the same position, still with a chunk of his head unaccounted for. Gus tried shaking him and talking to him but nothing seemed to be working. He really was dead. How the fuck was this possible? Why was it possible?

Gus took Kovac's wallet and personal items just in case and ran as fast as he could through the dark until he got to their place. He called Tallulah and told her what had happened. She drove over there in the middle of the night until her headlights came upon Kovac's dead body on the road. No one had discovered it yet. She picked up Gus and together they got rid of Kovac's body. He wouldn't tell me how.

Neither of them understood what happened. They hadn't a clue as to why Kovac was suddenly capable of dying. Obviously, it didn't apply to Gus because he recovered and apparently Tallulah had tried killing herself that night with no luck, so what was different?

Gus said nothing seemed to change for either of them. The only new development he could think of was that Kovac had finally heard from his estranged daughter in Georgia that day. He had written her a heartfelt letter asking for a chance to be a part of her life and she had responded positively to it. Gus said he'd never seen Kovac so happy. He'd actually had never seen Kovac happy but he was floating on air that night. That's why they were out so late. They were celebrating Kovac's reconnection with his daughter, Patricia. It's all Kovac ever hoped for and now it would never happen.

I'd bet a million dollars Tallulah is home right now analyzing this unexpected turn of events over and over in the hopes of figuring out what made Kovac vulnerable. I know I am, so her brain must be working overtime. Poor Kovac. He finally gets a sliver of hope and it's taken away in the middle of nowhere darkness by a couple of stupid kids who will never understand, nor care about, exactly what they took from him.

VINCENT VIÑAS

I can't stop thinking about Tallulah.

I Still Want To Help Her,

Guy

JULY 14TH

To My Dear Family,

Have you ever had so much on your mind you were certain it would crash like an overworked computer? That's how the week's been for me. One thought away from a complete system meltdown at all times. Friar. Kovac. Tallulah. Neither one of them could escape my brain. Mostly Tallulah.

The advice that I'd swear Friar gave me in that embalming room circled my head until it made perfect sense. I could help Tallulah but at the expense of my own happiness. We didn't really want the same thing and I had to make a decision. I could either move on and pray that the sadness of being rejected by her gives me the inspiration I need to achieve what I initially wanted-- death. Or I could figure out how to give her what she wants and we both win. I don't win in the way I'd like to at this point but I'd still take it. I couldn't go on living without her anyway. No sense in lying to myself anymore.

I found myself on the roof of the glass factory again. Not with the intentions of jumping. Just to take all these thoughts in. "I knew I'd find you here." I felt like I hadn't heard her voice in a hundred years. I couldn't turn around yet because I knew if I saw her, I'd break down right away.

Why's that?

249

"You always come here when things get to be too much."

I guess.

"This is where we first met."

Oh.

"It really is a great view from up here. Isn't it?"

Yeah.

"You know, we were always so caught up in dying while being at this factory that I rarely ever noticed the beauty of this place. Well... there was that one night we had. That one... perfect night."

Tallulah, I--

As I turned to face her I was interrupted by the sight of a large bandage on her arm. I've never seen her wearing one. Why would she? She always recovers right away. I asked her about the bandage and she told me she had been having one of her episodes and accidentally cut herself with some broken glass.

It was a nasty looking gash and she said it wouldn't stop bleeding. This is strange because you always heal immediately. It was barely audible but I heard her, very softly, say, "I know." Our eyes finally met and I noticed the relief and sadness in hers. She'd never worn this expression before. I understood though as the realization swept over me. She didn't have to say it but she did anyway.

"I think I can die now."

How?

"I don't know exactly, but I'm thinking...I'm thinking maybe it's because I have something to lose now. I mean, what the hell did Kovac have to live for until he heard from his daughter? Now he's dead. Maybe that's how it works. Maybe your love was meant to save me after all, because life has always been worthless to me. Perhaps because I felt that way about it, life wouldn't let me escape. Then you came along and loved me. You loved me in all the ways I didn't think people were capable of doing anymore. And now that I love you with all of my heart, life has made sure that I'm so fucked up inside that I can't possibly enjoy it. Not after everything I've been through."

Tallulah...I love you more than I can possibly describe. You're the best thing that has ever happened to me. As painful as it is to think—and as painful as it will be to do--I know what needs to be done and I won't let you down. I will end your suffering.

We stood on that roof forever--our bodies; our lips; our souls as one. Tomorrow, I will show Tallulah just how much I love her. Tomorrow, all of her pain and all of her worries get laid to rest. Tomorrow, Tallulah Leigh, the most beautiful woman in the world, will finally die.

A Total Mess,

Guy

FAREWELL, MY REASON FOR LIVING

JULY 16TH

To My Dear Family,

It is with a pain in my heart I wouldn't wish on my worst enemy that I write these words. I was hoping to feel numb but I don't and the sadness is kicking my ass. If it were possible to choke to death on one's own tears I'd be dead right now. I want to tell you what happened because this may very well be the last time I write to you.

I didn't want to be spotted by anyone in Tallulah's neighborhood so I had her meet me in a remote area. There was a nearby swamp that we pushed her car into. She thought it'd be better to destroy her license plate and sink the buggy rather than ditch it someplace where cops would find it and try to find its previous owner. She drove one of those Volkswagen Beetles. The newer ones. I don't know if I've ever told you that. Aside from it being black, it didn't really go with her personality but she liked it.

We got into my car and headed over to the funeral home. Luckily there was a thick overcast so it was already dark. I wanted to go as unnoticed as possible. We also lucked out as there was nothing scheduled for that evening, work-wise. I prayed that Bates wouldn't call me, saying there was a body I had to pick up somewhere that night. I went inside first to make sure no one was around. There was always the chance Tim or Richard could be using the rare downtime to tidy up.

The place was empty but I snuck Tallulah in any way as if it were the middle of the day. I kept almost all of the lights off too, only turning on one at any given time if possible. I was taking a huge risk, possibly ruining Bates' business in addition to losing my job and going to jail for the rest of my life, but I didn't care. Losing my job and getting arrested doesn't scare me because how much longer can I expect to live anyway. I just didn't want to ruin things for Bates. He was an asshole, but he was pretty fair and always showed me more respect than I thought possible from him.

I took Tallulah to the crematorium and she made me turn around so she could change. I changed as well, into my usual black suit. I wanted to prep the cremator so I had to promise not to sneek-a-peek at her while I did this. Our cremator has a feature that doesn't let you open its door until it reaches operating temperature. I couldn't afford to waste any time with this so I wanted everything ready to go.

I prepared all I could and just stood there, with my back to Tallulah as she finished getting ready. A few times I thought I would hyperventilate and pass out from anxiety. What was about to happen was bad enough without the extra nervousness of being caught. I suddenly froze in place. It was time. Then came the music.

The dark, brooding opening of Dido's Lament menaced the room with its over-powering sense of dread. I couldn't turn around. I just couldn't. It was too hard. When I am laid... No! This couldn't really be happening. ...am laid in earth. I told myself not to cry yet. I didn't want Tallulah to feel guilty for her decision. I agreed to do this and I wanted the last thing for her to feel was the love that made this possible. Not the hurt it would cause.

May my wrongs create... Her thin arms slid around my waist from behind as she hugged me. I gently placed my hands on top of hers. She began to sob softly as she rested her head on my shoulder. No trouble... "I'm gonna miss you so much, Guy."

No trouble in thy breast... I'm going to miss you too, Tallulah. I can't even tell you how lucky I feel to have met you. She placed her hands on my shoulders and made me turn to face her. When I am laid... Like me, she was wearing the same outfit she wore for our Funeral Portrait. She looked so absolutely beautiful I thought I would die on the spot from the sudden rush of blood throughout my body. ...am laid in earth.

Tallulah thought it only appropriate to die in that dress, while listening to the lament on the same radio in which we had first heard it together, that night on the factory roof. I didn't even realize she had brought the radio. May my wrongs create... We kissed with a passion that was surreal in its power. Soon afterwards our foreheads came to rest against one another. The song finished and restarted again without a word from either of us. All we could do was stand there in our embrace, staring into each other's tear-soaked eyes. ...No trouble.

We kissed some more during which Tallulah broke down, crying as painfully as one could. "I'm sorry. I am so sorry. I love you more than anything that could be loved. Please, always remember how much I love you." How could I ever forget? ...no trouble in thy breast. I will feel her love for the rest of my life and all throughout my death. I will always remember my Tallulah. Remember me...

It was so hard to let go but I knew if we didn't act soon I would never have enough time to do what I had to do before someone came in the next morning. With strength I didn't know I had, I released Tallulah so that she could lie down on one of the tables. Remember me... While she did this I retrieved the means of her demise. Tallulah had brought along a syringe that would serve as a lethal injection. I didn't ask her what was in it and I didn't care. ...but ah! forget my fate.

I walked over to the table and she was looking up at me with the sort of strained sympathetic smile you give someone as you watch them suffer. Remember me... The tears were now running down the side of her face towards her ears. I leaned over to kiss her again but not for too long because my will was deteriorating rapidly. Remember me... Tallulah...my dear, Tallulah...you are the best thing that has ever happened to me and I will miss you for as long as the human spirit can exist. I only hope that the love and happiness I couldn't give you in life will always be with you in death. ...but ah! forget my fate.

I couldn't think about it. Remember me... Not for half a second. I had to just do it and I did. I injected the contents of the syringe into her arm and took hold of her hand. She squeezed it at first but before long I could feel it loosening its grasp on me more and more. Her eyes, which were fixed on me initially, slowly closed as the lids became heavy. Her breathing decreased and soon stopped altogether. Remember me...

Tallulah Leigh, the woman who went through Hell to find a love she couldn't enjoy waiting for her on the other side, was now dead. ...but ah! Permanently.

...forget my fate.

I needed some time to grieve. No one could just go on with their tasks after what I had went through. How often does someone put the person they love the most to death? My God she was so beautiful.

I carefully placed Tallulah in one of our cardboard containers, which was already sitting on the charger. That's one of those motorized trolleys. I took off her earrings and put them in my pocket. She wasn't wearing any other jewelry. I put the rest of her other clothes and belongings in the container as well. The only other thing I kept was the radio. Finally, I placed a bouquet of flowers in her hands. I think she would have liked that.

THE FUNERAL PORTRAIT

She looked so peaceful lying there. It even almost seemed like she was smiling with the slightest bit of subtlety. At last she got what she wished for. And as much as it hurt to be the one that made it happen, I wouldn't have wanted it any other way. With that I opened the cremator door and had the charger slide the container that held Tallulah into the retort.

For the next two hours I sat there, crying and listening to Dido's Lament over and over. I couldn't believe she was gone. I can't. I might never come to terms with it. She was gone though and she definitely wouldn't be coming back this time.

Once the furnace had done its job, I swept all the bone fragments out of the retort. Sorting through her remains was without a doubt the most disturbing aspect of this whole ordeal. Seeing her little pieces of bone made it more real. I came very close to vomiting on them, which would have been catastrophic to me.

I put the fragments in the cremulator, which I mentioned to you once before and eventually, all that was left of Tallulah was in a small cardboard box which I held in my hands. It's always amazing to me that someone can live this whole life, affecting so many people along the way and in the end are nothing but dust in a small container.

I cleaned up as quickly as I could. I was pretty sure no one would notice that I was there or that the furnace had been used. Bates probably already got the message I left him saying that I wasn't feeling well so if anything came up today to call Devlin. It's now 9:29 AM and I still haven't been to sleep. I've been sitting here writing to you with Tallulah's boxed up remains beside me. I don't know when I'll be able to go to sleep again. I might never.

How would you expect me to ever close my eyes again and not see her face? This was supposed to be an arrangement. I kill her. Guilt kills me. In all honesty, I never really thought the guilt would give me the extra push I needed to die as well but after tonight I can already feel the guilt tightening around my neck like a noose. There is no way I will still be alive by this time tomorrow.

I love you and I'm sorry.
So Very Sorry,

Guy

SO THIS IS CLOSURE?

JULY 18TH

To My Dear Family,

Another day goes by and I'm still here. I didn't intend to be. It's been less than forty-eight hours since Tallulah's been gone and it feels like a lifetime. I love her so much. I hope wherever she is, she couldn't see my reaction to her death. I probably looked like such a blubbering fool that she wouldn't be able to enjoy her release from all her mortal suffering. I've never felt such pain in all my life. I truly believe people can die from heartache, because what I felt wasn't only mental, it was physical. The unbearable hurt, not only from missing her but knowing I'm the one that killed her, was ripping at me in every direction like a bunch of barbed hooks from Hell. I truly believed this agony would kill me for sure--but sometimes extraordinary things happen.

Shortly after my previous letter there was a knock at the door. You had already left for work, Bruno, and I didn't want to answer it. I didn't want to see or talk to anyone. I have to admit, I thought it could very well be the police looking to question me but no one knew what had happened at the funeral home. Not even Gus knew of our plans or that Tallulah could die and I will never tell him. I hope to never see that man again.

After whoever was knocking left I crept towards the window and was able to just catch a glimpse of their car--a postal jeep. I wasn't expecting any packages but I opened the front door and there was a small box, sitting there with my name on it. Before I could even bend down to pick it up a couple of sudden tears fell from my eyes and hit just to the side of the address label. It was from Tallulah.

I took it inside and spent the next hour just staring at the package without opening it. I was terrified to see what was inside. It felt like Tallulah reached out to me from the beyond and if I opened the box that would be it. There'd be no more contact with her ever again. I know she wanted me to have whatever was in the package but I wasn't ready to say goodbye for good.

Finally, I decided to open the box but not at home. I wanted to open it somewhere I could be alone. With all the animals, I never really feel completely alone in the house. So, I grabbed the package as well as the box of Tallulah's remains and got in my car. A little while later I was on the roof of the glass factory overlooking where I should have died countless times. It was a beautiful, warm but not overly hot, summer day. Before he died, I would be sure to find Mr. Friar on the side of the road with his peaches on a day like this. Such a wonderful day and there I was with a wretched face that was a mix of stress, sleep deprivation and misery.

I couldn't prolong it anymore. She had sent me this package for a reason and I'd be dishonoring her memory if I just stared at it for the next twenty years without opening it. I took several really deep breaths and opened the box. My heart sank when I viewed the contents. There was a box of chewy cinnamon candy. It had the old packaging like the kind they sell at Cracker Barrel. Where we first kissed. My Zippo lighter was in there too. The first thing we ever shared. Tallulah had had it engraved. It now said From T to G on it. It wasn't a gift from Constance anymore as far as I was concerned, it was a gift from Tallulah and I clutched it so tightly in my hand I'm amazed it didn't break.

There was also a picture I don't remember taking and with good reason. It was a close-up of my face and I was definitely sleeping. Tallulah's face was next to mine, giving me a kiss on the cheek. The angle would suggest that she took the picture herself. I felt there was something significant about the shirt she was wearing and then I suddenly remembered the one and only time she had worn it around me. The day we first made love.

There was a second picture I don't remember taking either, also with good reason. It was of the glass factory I currently occupied. This photo looked to be taken from a distance and upon closer inspection I noticed Tallulah and I standing by the ledge of the roof in it. The first day we met. She must have had Kovac or Gus take this for her with a zoom lens. I

261

wondered how many times she had watched me through that lens prior to that day. The final picture, which was in an antique 5x7 frame, made me swallow hard as I felt I couldn't breathe upon viewing it.

It was the Funeral Portrait.

How beautiful my Tallulah looked in that dress. How peaceful and innocent, lying in that casket with me beside her. How I loved her at that moment. How I love her now. I will love her always. She even included another copy of it that would fit in my wallet. It was awhile before I could even look at the note that accompanied all of this.

Dear Guy,

I will always be grateful to you for what you've given me. You've saved my life the way it needed to be saved. I only hope by doing so, I will in turn save yours the way it needs to be as well. Your life needs to be lived, my love. It's not too late for you. Any man that can penetrate this girl's heart the way you did deserves to share that love with someone who can really enjoy and cherish it, the way I wish I could. I love you tremendously and will miss you through all of eternity. Please, take care of yourself, my darling. I hope we find each other much earlier the next time around.

Live your life.

Love,

Tallulah

THE FUNERAL PORTRAIT

I didn't think I'd ever stop crying. Not while I read the note over and over, countless times. Not while I scattered her ashes upon the roof and over the ledge. Not while I set the box that held the residue of her remains on fire and watched it burn up completely. Not while I stared, transfixed, at our Funeral Portrait. I spent all day on the rooftop until the sky began its daily retreat to darkness.

It was time to leave now--to say goodbye. I stood up and looked over the surrounding area. The first stars of the night were already twinkling in the sky. She would have found it to be very beautiful.

I put everything she sent me back into its box for safe keeping, except for the small Funeral Portrait. I got my wallet out of my back pocket and opened it. The picture of Constance and me was still in there so I pulled it out of the plastic holder and held it for one last look. This used to be me. That me is dead now. He died today on that rooftop amongst Tallulah's ashes. He needed to die.

I lit the picture of Constance and I with my lighter and the flame ate it up instantly until it was gone. The small Funeral Portrait slid into the vacant picture slot perfectly. That's where it will stay to always remind me that I was once dead. To remind me that sometimes love can reanimate the cold-hearted; the empty-hearted. And sometimes love, real honest to God love, means being able to let go. Although she's gone, Tallulah wants me to live my life...

...and that's exactly what I'm going to do.

With All My Love,

Guy

THE END

NOTE FROM THE AUTHOR

NATIONAL SUICIDE PREVENTION LIFELINE

1-800-273-TALK (8255)

suicidepreventionlifeline.org

This is a work of fiction that mixes elements of comedy with a dark subject matter in order to tell a story. Even though real depression is by no means a laughing matter, I feel it is important to find humor as often as possible wherever we can in life, even in the unlikeliest of places. People always say smile and the world smiles with you. Cry and you cry alone. Well, the world may not always smile with you but you should never have to cry alone. If you or anyone you know is suffering from depression or suicidal thoughts, help is always available. Please contact the National Suicide Prevention Lifeline. They will be there to help you any time of day.

ACKNOWLEDGEMENTS

This book has traveled a long and dismal road in order to be in your hands today. I'd like to thank the individuals who have made the journey less painful.

I've had many wonderful teachers in my life all worth mentioning but the two who inspired me the most to write are Eric Friar and Barbara Peiser. Being the occasional serial napper in school, I definitely never felt compelled to hide behind a text book and sleep during their lessons.

My family deserves tremendous thanks, not only for letting me watch horror movies and read Stephen King novels when I was still in elementary school but for always encouraging a creative atmosphere. They also deserve credit for tolerating my life-long—for lack of a better term—"quirky" behavior, like the time I literally wanted to be Michael Jackson when I was four or when I spent an entire year behaving like Curly from The Three Stooges when I was nine.

I must give my brother, Victor Viñas, Jr. extra thanks for the snazzy cover artwork as well as George E. Wright, Jr. for the original book cover when I had self-published The Funeral Portrait as an e-book only. That cover really kicked me in the ass to get this book "out there."

Although we only worked on screenplays and short films together, Brian W. Smith—in between many glorious viewings of John Carpenter's Halloween--has taught me more about writing than he even knows. I can only hope to replicate just a little of his magic in my own work.

If you are in the Funeral Home business you will no doubt notice that I've taken certain liberties in regards to procedures. However, my descriptions would be outrageously inaccurate if not for the invaluable help of Mike Hodges and Arnold Edwards. Thank you for sharing your insights with me.

Very special thanks to Todd Smith and Jasan Stepp from Dog Fashion Disco for the inspiration and the lyrics. Your merch guy at the show said your large band shirts ran big but I'm still trying to squeeze into it years later. One day chocolate bars will lose their appeal and the shirt will fit.

I'd also like to send tremendous thanks to Ashley Howie and William Gardner at Ink Smith Publishing for taking a chance on a book that no one else knew what to do with.

Finally, a super ginormous, TARDIS full of purple tulips, thank you to my wife, Megan, for always appreciating how far I'm willing to go to get a laugh out of her; being a positive beacon on the rare occasions I'm convinced the universe is against me and for putting up with the whole smegging mess of a person I had to become to write this book. Smoke me a kipper. I'll be back for breakfast!

-- V.V.

VINCENT VIÑAS

CPSIA information can be obtained at www.ICGtesting.com
Printed in the USA
BVOW02s0934260314

348833BV00001B/97/P

9 781939 156105